Moon Cakes to Maize

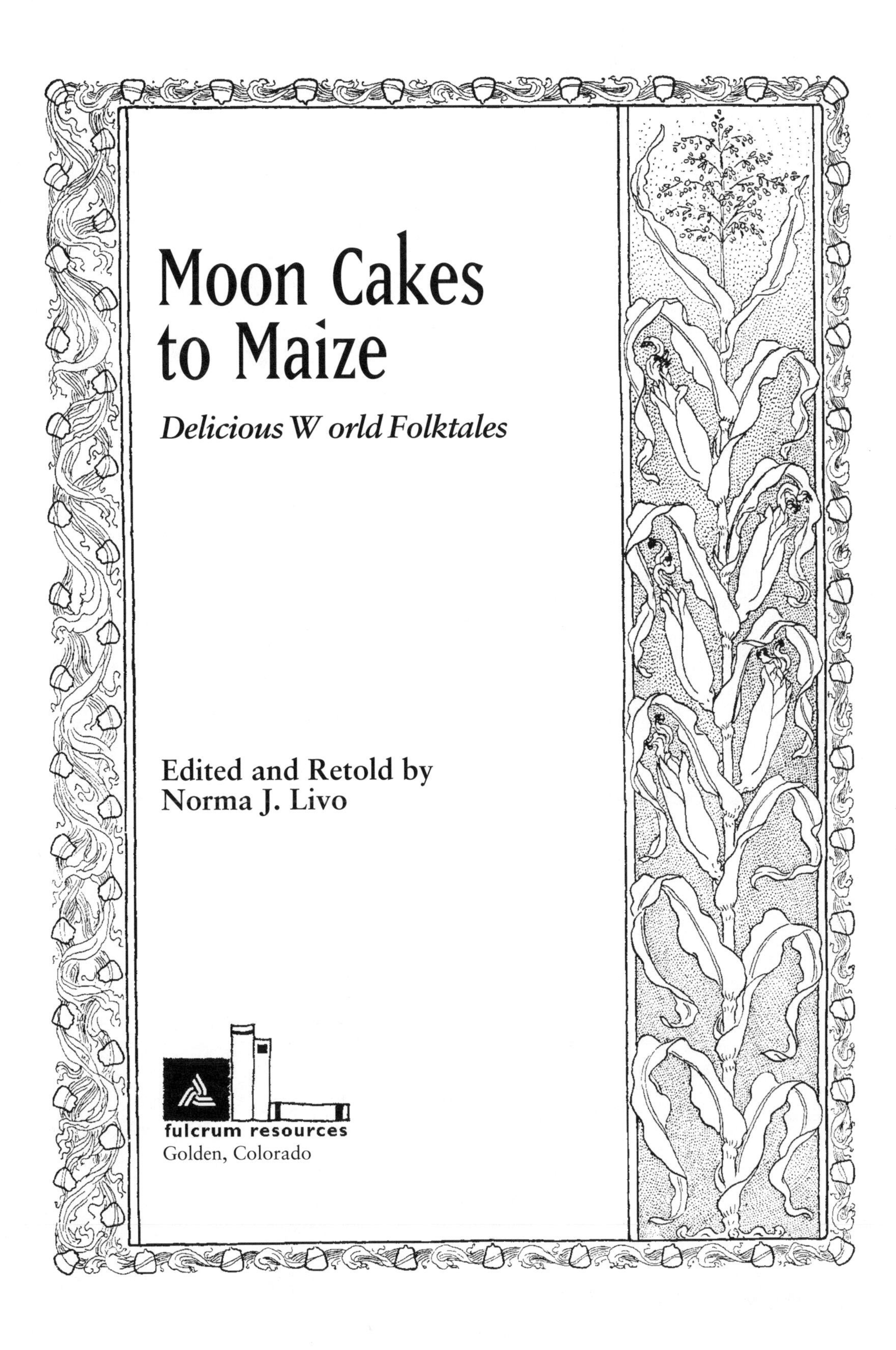

Moon Cakes to Maize

Delicious W orld Folktales

Edited and Retold by
Norma J. Livo

fulcrum resources
Golden, Colorado

Library of Congress Cataloging-in-Publication Data
Moon cakes to Maize : delicious world folktales / edited and retold by Norma J. Livo.
p. cm.
Includes bibliographical references.
ISBN 1-55591-973-1
1. Food—Folklore. I. Livo, Norma J., 1929– .
GR498.M66 1999
398.27—dc21 98–33373
CIP

Book design by Alyssa Pumphrey

Printed in the United States of America
0 9 8 7 6 5 4 3 2 1

Fulcrum Publishing
350 Indiana Street, Suite 350
Golden, Colorado 80401-5093
(800) 992-2908 • (303) 277-1623
website: www.fulcrum-resources.com
e-mail: fulcrum@fulcrum-resources.com

To all of my amazing family members
who are truly the spice of life!

Contents

Acknowledgments

I wish to acknowledge the world of stories related to food for the mind and imagination. Special thanks to Suzanne Barchers, Acquisitions Editor with Fulcrum Publishing, for her suggestions and ability to cook up good books.

Also, grateful acknowledgment is made for permission to use the following copyrighted tales: "Wolf Helper" from *By Cheyenne Campfires* by George Bird Grinnell, New Haven, Conn: Yale University Press, 1962; "The Modern Little Red" reprinted by permission from *Nation's Business,* July 1970, copyright 1970, U.S. Chamber of Commerce; "The Magic Tablecloth" taken from "The Stolen Turnips, the Magic Tablecloth, the Sneezing Goat, and the Wooden Whistle" from *Old Peter's Russian Tales* by Arthur Ransome, Dover Publications Inc., 1969; "Jack and the Beanstalk" from *English Fairy Tales,* collected by Joseph Jacobs, Dover Publications Inc., 1967; "The Story of the Three Bears" from *English Fairy Tales,* collected by Joseph Jacobs, Dover Publications Inc., 1967; and "Scrapefoot" from *More English Fairy Tales* by Joseph Jacobs, Dover Publications Inc., 1967.

Introduction

Moon Cakes to Maize: Delicious World Folktales is a story anthology connected with the theme of food. Stories throughout the world are full of poor folks who are hungry, royalty and the rich having feasts, explanations for how some foods came to people, and magical ways to obtain food. Everyone needs to eat! Everyone has been hungry at some time. We need food regularly, and I believe we need stories to feed us, too. Stories sustain our sense of imagination.

Foods and cooking appeal to the senses. Smells, sights, textures, tastes, sounds, and memories are involved with foods and eating. Family gatherings and celebrations usually involve food and they make memories of good times and social sharing.

Our language is full of terms about food and cooking. You can boil with rage, you can burn with love, you can cook someone's goose by getting him in hot water or in a pickle. Dad forks over money, Mom dishes out advice, and your last assignment was a piece of cake. We also talk about the spice of life.

Because sustenance can pertain not only to food, but to stories, an appealing and appropriate example can be found in one of Winnie the Pooh's predicaments. In the story, Pooh gets stuck in Rabbit's hole after eating too much honey. The bear and his friends decide he will just have to stay stuck there and eat no food until he is able to wiggle out of the hole. Pooh sighs and then says, "Then would you read a Sustaining Book such as would help and comfort a Wedged Bear in Great Tightness?" *Moon Cakes to Maize* can provide such sustaining possibilities.

This book includes suggestions and activities to extend the experience of the stories in a "Food for Thought" section at the end of each part. *Moon Cakes to Maize* is intended for teachers, librarians, and story lovers. It could also be a companion book to *Storybook Stew* by Suzanne I. Barchers and Peter J. Rauen (Golden, Colo.: Fulcrum, 1996).

A wholesome meal can truly satisfy hunger, and a good story is a very satisfying experience.

Bon Appétit!

Part One

Legends and Beliefs

Moon Cakes
(China)

A GREAT HORDE OF MONGOL RIDERS swept across China's northern border early in the thirteenth century. Behind them they left countless dead, plundered villages, sacked cities, and devastated countryside. Ju Yuan-jang, a Buddhist priest, the son of a poor peasant family, became the unexpected brave leader of his people. He traded his priestly robes for a soldier's uniform when he could no longer stand what the cruel conquerors inflicted on his people. He secretly organized a group of loyal men for an army. The men were willing to give up their lives to follow their priest-turned-warrior, General Ju. He and his army battled the Mongols for twelve years, accomplishing the impossible. With each victory, Ju's fame spread.

His troops faced the awesome task of recapturing the walled city of Feng Yang. Feng Yang was situated between a wide, fast-flowing river and an imposing mountain range. This location presented General Ju with a dilemma. How could he possibly cross the river to attack without being seen by Mongol guards on duty at the top of the city walls? Attack from the mountains would also leave his men in a trap as they worked their way through a narrow pass. General Ju conferred with his chief aide, Liu Bowen. These two men were equally matched in bravery and determination.

The biggest problem was not knowing what was happening within the walled city. They needed this formation to design a battle plan. Finally Liu volunteered to enter the city to study the Mongol's strength as well as to investigate if the people themselves could be counted on to rise up. General Ju knew that the gates to the city were constantly guarded. They had to figure out some plan that would get Liu safely into the city.

Liu decided to go in disguised as an ordinary peddler with a sack of leeks. General Ju worried for his safety, but Liu insisted that he could do it. And so, Liu went to the city gates where a guard stopped him and examined his sack. The guard waved Liu into the city when he got a whiff of the strong-smelling garden herb. Inside the city, Liu went to the marketplace. He knew that this would be the place where he could talk with the people. The marketplace was crowded with farmers who had come to sell their produce. Liu imitated the other merchants, opening his sack and calling out to customers to come and buy his leeks. Those that did stop by his sack haggled with him over the price. Liu observed that everyone was being thrifty with their money. When he tried to talk with them, the people were uncomfortable and even seemed afraid.

At the end of the day Liu had only managed to sell half of his herbs. He recognized a man who had come to look at the leeks as Chang Li-bo, from the village of Fu Shan. They had been boyhood friends. They exchanged greetings and brought each other up to the present with the happenings of their families. Chang invited Liu to come to his house, which Liu was pleased to do. Chang's small home was in a poor part of Feng Yang. There were only two rooms in it. Chang's wife and fifteen-year-old daughter greeted Liu and presented the men with tea. It was natural for these two men to talk openly with each other.

Chang told Liu that the Mongols mistreated his people, abused them, and stole from them, and worst of all, killed them for no provocation. In fact, the Mongol general had just issued a new decree stating that one out of every twenty families was ordered to house a Mongol soldier. They were instructed to house, feed, and obey them. Chang and his family had to give up one of their own rooms to a Mongol. They lived in fear of what would happen to them.

Liu felt safe telling his old friend that a Chinese army was just outside the city prepared to take over the city. Liu went through the city gates before they were locked for the night, safe in the knowledge that Chang had sworn secrecy. Liu reported back to General Ju what he had heard, seen, and learned in the city. The two men sat outside the general's tent and discussed battle plans. It was a night on which the moon hung like a lantern, casting long shadows that moved with the breeze. As Liu gazed at the sky, he was struck with a plan. The Mid-Autumn Festival would be celebrated in a few days and everyone would be eating the traditional moon cakes. With this inspiration, he explained what they would do.

Step by step he went through his plan with General Ju. For the next two days the army cooks mixed, kneaded, and baked thousands of moon cakes. The very last batch of moon cakes that was taken from the stoves were decorated with a pea-sized bright red mark. When all of the moon cakes had cooled, they were packed into four large baskets. The day before the Mid-Autumn Festival, Liu and three of the army's bravest soldiers dressed up in dirty, ill-fitting pants and raggedy jackets full of patches. They went to the city gates. Each of them had a basket strapped to his back, and they walked through the gates like ordinary peddlers. They set up a stall in the city market and placed three of the baskets on a crude counter, hiding the fourth one under it.

The tantalizing smell of the freshly baked pastries with their delicious sweet bean-paste attracted buyers. Whenever someone bought a few cakes, a soldier would reach into the basket under the counter and take a cake with a red mark on it. He would hand it to the buyer and tell him that it was a bonus. "It has a very special filling that you will surely like. May you be blessed with good fortune on the day of the Mid-Autumn Festival," was said as each special moon cake was given.

Of course, the Mongols were curious about why this stall was doing so much business, so Liu graciously offered them a few cakes. The rude Mongols grabbed as many of the moon cakes as they could and went on through the market.

Chang came to the stall late in the day. Liu motioned him to be quiet and took him aside. Liu gave Chang a bag of moon cakes and told him to open the one that had a red dot as soon as he returned to his house. Liu assured Chang that he would know what to do next.

People being people, those who had been given a moon cake with a red mark did not wait for the Festival to taste them. As they bit into the moon cakes they discovered tiny pieces of rolled paper with a written message: "On the evening of the Mid-Autumn Festival, when you see bonfires in the hills above the city, kill the Mongol soldier in your house. Prepare for an avenging Chinese army to arrive."

Word flew as quick as the wind throughout the city. Since the Mongols had taken all weapons from the people, the people used anything they could find as weapons: fence staves, stones, pots, and anything else they could find. Festival day brought an early close to the shops. Everyone had hurried home and only the Mongol guards were left on the streets, in their usual patrol. Just after nightfall huge fires appeared in the hills. The signal to attack had been given. The Mongol soldiers never had a chance to escape the fury of the people. After the Mongols were put to death, the people fought their way toward the city gates. Within a very short time the streets were littered with Mongol bodies. The Mongol general ordered his guards to leave their posts on top of the city walls and join the forces fighting at the city gates.

Tall ladders were placed against the walls by General Ju's men. Ju's soldiers climbed to the top and pulled up the ladders which they then swung over to the other side. The battle raged on. Chang finally reached the city gates and flung them open. In flooded Liu and his troops. Wave after wave of Chinese soldiers charged through the heavy wooden gates and battled the Mongols. Eventually the Mongol general surrendered and was led away in chains.

To this day it is said that the capture of the walled city of Feng Yang was an incredible victory that destroyed Mongol power. General Ju rose to great glory and was seated on the Imperial Throne as the first Ming Emperor. The dynasty he founded lasted for three hundred blessed years. Today, as they have done for centuries, the Chinese people eat moon cakes during the Mid-Autumn Festival. It is traditional to decorate them with a spot of red coloring in honor of Ju's great victory. To eat a moon cake is a double treat—the delicious sweetness of the filling satisfies the taste and the red symbol satisfies the soul.

The Wolf Helper

*(Cheyenne)**

AFTER THE SAND CREEK MASSACRE WAS OVER, and the troops had gone, there were two women left alive. In 1902 these women were still living. One was named Two She-Wolf Woman, and the other, Standing in Different Places Woman. They were sisters, and each had a little daughter, one ten years old and one of six years. One of their husbands was badly wounded and likely to die, and he told them they must leave him and go home to the camp, so that they might save themselves and their children. They started. They had no food, and no implements except their knives and a little short-handled ax. They had their robes.

They traveled on and on, until they reached the Smoky Hill River. Here they found many rose berries, and they pounded them up with the little ax and ate them. After they had pounded the rose berries they made flat cakes of them to give to the children, and started on. They did not know where the camp was, and did not know where to go. They just followed the river down.

One night after they had been traveling for six or seven days, they went into a little hole in the bluff for shelter, for it was very cold. They were sitting up, one robe under them, with the other in front of them, and with the children lying between them. In the middle of the night something came into the hole and lay down by them, and when this thing had come near to them, standing between them and the opening of the hole, they saw that it was a big wolf, and were afraid of it; but it lay down quietly.

Next morning they started on, and the wolf went with them, walking not far to one side of them. Their feet were sore, for their moccasins were

*From *By Cheyenne Campfires* by George Bird Grinnell. New Haven, Conn.: Yale University Press, 1962.

worn out, and they often stopped to rest. When they did so the wolf lay down nearby. At one of these halts the elder woman spoke to the wolf, just as she would talk to a person. She said to him: "O Wolf, try to do something for us. We and our children are nearly starved." When she spoke to him, the wolf seemed to listen and rose up on his haunches and looked at her, and when she stopped speaking he rose to his feet and started off toward the north. It was the early part of the winter, but there was no snow on the ground.

The women sat there resting, for they were weak and tired and footsore. They saw the wolf pass out of sight over the hill, and after a time they saw him coming back. He came toward them, and when he was close to them they could see that his mouth and jaws were covered with blood. He stepped in front of them and turned his head and looked back in the direction from whence he had come. The women were so weak and stiff they could hardly get up, but they rose to their feet. When they stood up the wolf trotted off to the top of the hill and stopped, looking back, and they followed him very slowly. When they reached the top of the hill they saw, down in the little draw behind, the carcass of a buffalo. In a circle around it sat many wolves. The wolf looked back at the women again, and then loped down toward the carcass. Now the women started to walk fast toward the carcass, for here was food. All the wolves still sat about; they were not feeding on the carcass.

When the women reached it they drew their knives and opened it. They made no fire, but at once ate the liver and tripe, and the fat about the intestines, without cooking, and gave food to the children. Then they cut off pieces of the meat, as much as they could carry, and made up packs and started on their way. As soon as they had left the carcass, all the wolves fell upon it and began to eat it quickly, growling and snarling at each other, and soon they had eaten it all. The big wolf ate with the other wolves. The women went on over the hill and stopped; they had eaten so much that they could not go far. In the evening, when the sun was low, one of the women said to the other, "Here is our friend again," and the wolf came trotting up to them.

Soon after he had joined them they started on to look for a hollow where they might sleep. The wolf traveled with them. When it grew dark they stopped, and the wolf lay near them. Every day they tried to find a place to camp where there were willows. They cut these and made a shelter of them, and covering it with grass, made a bed of grass, then put down their robes and covered themselves with grass. So they were well sheltered.

One morning as they were going along they looked over the hill and saw in the bottom below them some ponies feeding. They started down to see whose they were, the wolf traveling along, but off to one side. Before they had come near to the horses two persons came up over a hill, and when these persons saw the women coming they sprang on their horses and rode away fast. The women walked on to the place where the men had been. Here there was a fire, and meat that the men had left: a tongue and other food roasting. The women took the meat and ate, then cut the tongue in two and gave the smaller end of it to the wolf, which had come up and was lying by the fire.

After they had finished eating they went on, soon coming to a big spring with a hollow nearby, a good place to camp. They were glad to find the place, for the sky looked as if it were going to snow. They made a house of willows and grass and covered it with bark from the trees. By this time they had become so accustomed to having the wolf with them that every night they made a bed near the door of the house, piling up grass for him to sleep on.

That night the women heard a noise down in the hollow, something calling like a big owl. Two She-Wolf Woman was watching; they were afraid during the night and used to take turns keeping watch. They could hear this thing breaking sticks as it walked about. The watcher awoke her sister, saying, "Wake up! Something is coming." The wolf now stood up, and soon he began to howl with a long, drawn-out cry, which was very dismal. Soon from all directions many wolves began to come to the place. After a little while the thing that was making the noise began to come closer, and when it did so all the wolves rushed toward it and began fighting it. The women seized their children and ran away into the night. They got far out on the level prairie and stopped there, for their feet were sore, and they were very tired. In the morning, just as day was breaking they saw the big wolf coming toward them. When he reached them he lay down.

The elder woman now spoke to him again, and said, "Wolf, take pity on us; help us to find the trail of our people." When she had ceased speaking, the wolf trotted away, leaving the women, and they followed on very slowly. Before long they saw him coming back toward them fast—loping. When he got to them they saw that he had in his mouth a big piece of dried meat. He dropped the meat in front of them. They seized the meat and divided it, and gave some of it to their children and ate of it themselves. The wolf did not lie down, but stood waiting, and when they had eaten, he led them to an old camp where there were sticks standing in the ground. On each stick hung a parfleche sack of meat. Their relations had left these things for them, knowing that they were lost and thinking that they might pass this way.

Now the women had plenty of food; they went to the water and built a shelter with a place in it for the wolf. That night it snowed. When they arose the snow was above their ankles. Again the woman spoke to the wolf, asking him to go and find their camp, and he went away. The women stayed there. The wolf was not gone a long time; he came back the same day. They were watching for him, for now they knew that he was their friend and that he was true; they knew that he would do something for them. The two women went to the top of the little hill nearby, and before night they saw the wolf coming. He came up to them and stopped, then began to look back. The women felt sure that he had found something, went back to their camp and got their children, and went to the wolf, who started back as he had come, traveling ahead of them. On the point of a high hill he stopped. When the women overtook him they looked down and saw a big Cheyenne camp on the river below. This was the head of the Republican River.

They went on down to the camp, to the lodge of Gray Beard. The wolf remained on the hill. After the women had eaten, the older woman took meat. She told the people that a wolf had led them to the camp and that she was going back to give him something to eat. She went back and gave the wolf the food. After he had eaten she said to him, "Now, you have brought us to the camp, you can go back to your old ways." Late that evening the woman went up on the hill again to see if the wolf was there, but he was gone. She saw his tracks going back the same way that he had come. This happened in the winter of 1864 and 1865. The women and one of the children are still alive.

Legend of the Rice Seed

*(Hmong of Southeast Asia)**

A POOR WIDOW, whose only child was a thirteen-year-old daughter, had to go daily to dig up wild tubers and yams near a large river in order to survive. One day the daughter disappeared and the distraught mother could not find her.

Later the mother was digging for food in the same area when she heard her daughter call out from the river. The daughter had married the Lord Dragon who lived in the river, and she invited her mother to come and visit her in the water.

After staying with them for a while, the mother longed to return home. The Lord Dragon gave her some magical rice seed specially packed in a leaf and a hollow reed, promising that if she planted it she would have more than enough to eat and drink.

The mother planted the seeds, and in time she had such a huge harvest of rice that she was unable to carry all of it home. She went to the river and asked the Lord Dragon what to do. "If there is too much rice," he replied, "stand in your field and whistle three times, then clap your hands three times."

The mother returned to her field and did as her son-in-law directed. Miraculously, the amount of rice diminished, and she carried home in one day all that was left.

To this day, her people continue to use a leaf and a hollow reed for their ceremonial rice seed, and they never clap their hands or whistle while in a rice field.

---

*From *Folk Stories of the Hmong* by Norma J. Livo and Dia Cha. Englewood, Colo.: Libraries Unlimited, 1991.

Why Farmers Have to Work So Hard

*(Hmong of Southeast Asia)**

LONG, LONG AGO, plants and animals of all kinds were able to talk. They used words just like we do today. Here is what happened.

Lou Tou and his wife Ntsee Tyee were the first people of the Hmong. When they came to the surface of the earth from a crack in the rocks on a mountainside, Lou Tou carried a flower with him.

Each day Lou Tou and Ntsee Tyee ate a few seeds from the flower, until one day they saw that the seeds would soon be all gone. So they decided to plant the few remaining seeds.

After some time, a single stalk of corn grew where they had planted the seeds. But this was a special corn stalk, because on it grew several different kinds of grain. There were an ear of corn with seven leaves, an ear of yellow sticky corn, an ear of early white corn, a larger ear of late white corn, and three ears with three different kinds of millet. The last ear of corn on the stalk was white sticky corn, and the tassel at the very tip of the stalk was covered with rice.

All the grains on the special corn stalk grew and ripened. The first to ripen was the seven-leaf corn, and it returned to Lou Tou and Ntsee Tyee's house. "Mama and Papa, if you please, open the door," it said.

Lou Tou and Ntsee Tyee looked at each other. They did not recognize the voice, so they replied, "We would be willing to open the door, but you must tell us who you are."

"I am the seven-leaf ear of corn. I am part of the flower you brought with you from inside the earth."

"Where are you going to stay if we let you come in?" asked Lou Tou.

---

*From *Folk Stories of the Hmong* by Norma J. Livo and Dia Cha. Englewood, Colo.: Libraries Unlimited, 1991, pp. 47–53.

"Since I am small and don't want to be cold, I would like to be hung from the ceiling joists under the attic platform."

Shortly after that, the yellow sticky corn ripened and came to the couple's door. "Mama and Papa, please open the door," it said.

"Yes, we will open the door, but who are you?" they asked.

The answer was, "We are part of the flower you brought from inside the earth."

"Where are you going to find room if we let you come in?" they asked again.

"We would like to hang under the attic floor, from the ceiling joists," answered the ears of yellow sticky corn. When the door was opened, they came in and were hung beside the ear of seven-leaf corn.

A few days later the early maturing corn asked to come into Lou Tou and Ntsee Tyee's house. "Who are you?" they asked the corn.

"We are part of the flower. We are the early corn," was the answer.

"Where do you want to be put?" the couple asked.

"Hang us under the attic floor," said the early corn. And so they were hung alongside the other corn.

Several days later, the late maturing corn came and said, "Mama and Papa, open the door for us."

"Who are you?" Lou Tou and his wife asked.

"We are part of the flower. We are the ears of late corn," came the reply.

"Where do you want to stay?" the couple asked.

"There are a lot of us. We want to stay in a special small room." So Lou Tou and Ntsee Tyee built a granary on tall poles, to keep the small room off the ground. That way the rats could not get to the room. There they stored the late maturing corn.

Shortly after they finished building the granary, the couple heard again, "Mama and Papa, please open the door."

"We will open the door, but who are you?"

"We are part of the flower. We are grains of millet. We have had a lot of trouble living and growing. Most of our grains died, but we have managed to come home," the millet said.

"Where do you want to stay?" asked the couple.

"We would like to stay in a basket up in the attic, right over the fireplace."

Lou Tou had to weave a basket to hold the millet. When he was finished, he put the millet in the basket in the attic.

A few days later, the grains of another kind of millet asked to come in. "Who are you?" asked Ntsee Tyee and Lou Tou.

"We are part of the flower. We are millet grains. Many of us had trouble growing and each cluster of us is only half filled out. We are ripe, though. Please let us come back home."

"Where do you want to stay?" the couple asked the millet.

"We would like to stay in a large storage basket." And so a large bamboo storage bin was made ready to hold the grain.

Several days later, the grains of rice arrived and asked, "If you please, Mama and Papa, open the door."

"Who are you?" demanded Lou Tou and his wife.

"We are part of the flower. We are ripe and want to come back home," the rice said.

"Where do you want to stay?" the couple asked the rice.

"We would like to stay in a large, strong basket."

So Lou Tou had to weave another basket like the large storage bin for the grains of rice.

Lou Tou and Ntsee Tyee now had all kinds of grain. They had all they needed to plant and grow crops to eat. That was the way it was on earth for a long time. The grains always came to the home of the farmer when they were ripe and ready to use.

Many, many years later, a Hmong farmer went out one day to clear land to make a new field to plant grain. First he cut down the bamboo and trees. They cried and cried without stopping.

Then he cut away all of the plants already growing on the ground and set fire to them. The fire spread to the whole field and all the plants, trees, and bamboo sobbed and wailed. They cried without stopping.

The Hmong farmer planted the field in rice and corn. A short time after he planted the grains, they sprouted all together and began to grow. But oh! When the little plants were as big as the curved feathers in a rooster's tail, all the wild plants began to grow back, too. The wild plants began hitting the rice and corn and breaking them down.

"This will never do," said the corn and rice. So they went and told the farmer what was happening. "Mr. Hmong farmer, you went out and planted us in the heart of the forest. Now the bamboo groves and trees that are growing there are banging into us and hitting us. They are breaking off our hands and our feet. Why did you plant us there? If you don't help us we won't survive."

The farmer told them, "Dear Corn and Rice, go and wait for seven days and I will come. In seven days I will come to where you live. I will make sure those wild plants won't hurt you anymore."

When the rice and corn got back to the forest field, they said to the wild plants and trees, "You better quit hitting and hurting us. We have a strong farmer who is going to come and see you. When he comes he will make trouble for you. There is no telling what he might do to you! We have told him all about you."

The bamboo, trees, and plants answered the grain, "If that is so, tell us what your farmer looks like."

"Our farmer is a man who wears a broad-brimmed, wool felt hat. His clothes are black and he carries a big knife. He will be puffing on a pipe. Just keep watching and when you see a man like that, he is the one," replied the grain.

The next day a tiger passed through the field. The bamboo, trees, vines, bushes, weeds, and grass started hitting the rice and corn and sneered, "Is this your owner?"

"No, it is not, no, it is not, no, it is not," chanted the rice and corn. "Not this one."

The very next day a bobcat sauntered by. While the bobcat passed, the wild plants began hitting the rice and corn again. "Is he the one?"

"No, he is not, no, he is not, no, he is not," came the reply. "Please, don't hit us like that! It hurts so much."

The third day a rat came scurrying through the field, pushing his way through the leaves and grass. The wild plants laughed and taunted, "Ha! Is this little creature with the long tail your chief? Your leader? Your owner?"

"No, he is not, no, he is not, no, he is not," whispered the rice and the corn.

"You are lucky, Corn and Rice, because if he is, we could just fall on him and crush him. He is so little we could easily take care of him!"

During the fourth day, a snorting bull came through the field. He was going to eat the grass plants, but the plants were rough and had stickers on them that hurt his mouth, so he went on. The wild plants asked, "Is this one your chief?"

"No, he is not, no, he is not, no, he is not," came the answer.

The fifth day a wolf went by. The wild plants asked, "Is this the one or not?"

"No, he is not the one either," groaned the rice and corn.

The sixth day a chicken flew over the field. "Ha, ha, ha! Is that your brave owner?" the wild plants taunted.

"No, he is not, no, he is not, no, he is not," was the reply.

At last the seventh day arrived. The Hmong farmer walked and walked and walked on his way to the field. He walked for half a day to get there. When he arrived the weeds and other harmful plants asked the corn and rice, "Is this your chief, your owner and protector?"

The rice and corn sighed with relief. "Yes, he is. He is the very one. Take a good look at him!"

The Hmong farmer began to chop the weeds and wild plants with his big knife. The wild plants all started crying at once, wailing and lamenting without end. The farmer sliced their necks so their heads fell off, PLOP! He cut them all off, all of the weeds in the whole field.

And so, at last the rice and corn grew and got big. The rice told the farmer, "Ah, Mr. Hmong farmer, you have helped us very much, in many, many ways. Now you can go home and rest. You planted us and took care of us, and now you can stay home. We will come to you when we are ripe. But you have one more thing to do. Make a granary for us to live in at your home. We will come to you on our own when we are fully grown."

So the farmer went home. He did nothing, however, but went straight to bed. He lazed around in bed for a long time. In fact, he stayed in bed so long that his ear became flat and stuck to his head.

When the rice and corn were fully grown they all came at once, like a stream of flowing water, to the farmer's home. But there was no place ready for them to stay. There were no storage house, no bins, no granary, nothing! That meant they would have to stay outside, and they would get wet and rot when it rained. The rats would be able to get at them and eat them. So the rice and corn told the farmer, "We have come to you as we promised. You do not have a place ready for us to stay. Since this is true, we will go back to the field and whenever you get hungry for something to eat, you will have to come and get us. Hereafter, you will have to work to bring us in."

And so the rice and corn plants went back out to the field in the middle of the forest and stayed there until the farmer came to get them. That is why, even today, Hmong farmers have to walk long distances to the fields and carry their harvests on their backs.

The Ear of Corn

(Brothers Grimm)

IN FORMER TIMES, when God himself still walked the earth, the fruitfulness of the soil was much greater than it is now. Then, the ears of corn did not bear fifty or sixty, but four or five hundredfold. Then the corn grew from the bottom to the very top of the stalk. The longer the stalk, the longer the ear. Men, however, are so made, that when they are too well off they no longer value the blessings that come from God, but grow indifferent and careless.

One day a woman was passing by a cornfield when her little child, who was running beside her, fell into a puddle and dirtied her frock. On this, the mother tore up a handful of the beautiful ears of corn, and cleaned the frock with them.

When the Lord saw that, He was angry and said, "Henceforth shall the stalks of corn bear no more ears. Men are no longer worthy of heavenly gifts." The bystanders who heard this were terrified and fell on their knees and prayed that He would still leave something on the stalks, even if the people were undeserving of it, for the sake of the innocent birds, which would otherwise starve. The Lord, who foresaw their suffering, had pity on them, and granted the request. So the ears were left as they now grow.

The Garden of Eden

(Genesis 3: 1–24)

Now the serpent was more subtle than the beast of the field, which the Lord God had made. And he said unto the woman, "Yea, hath God said, Ye shall not eat of every tree of the garden?"

And the woman said unto the serpent, "We may eat of the fruit of the trees of the garden:

But of the fruit of the tree which is in the midst of the garden, God hath said, Ye shall not eat of it, neither shall ye touch it, lest ye die."

And the serpent said unto the woman, "Ye shall not surely die:

For God doth know that in the day ye eat thereof, then your eyes shall be opened, and ye shall be as gods, knowing good and evil."

And when the woman saw that the tree was for food, and that it was pleasant to the eyes, and a tree to be desired to make one wise, she took of the fruit thereof, and did eat, and gave also unto her husband with her; and he did eat.

And the eyes of them both were opened, and they knew that they were naked; and they sewed fig leaves together, and made themselves aprons.

And they heard the voice of the Lord God walking in the garden in the cool of the day: and Adam and his wife hid themselves from the presence of the Lord God amongst the trees of the garden.

And the Lord God called unto Adam, and said unto him, "Where art thou?"

And he said, "I heard thy voice in the garden, and I was afraid, because I was naked: and I hid myself."

And the Lord God said, "Who told thee that thou wast naked? Hast thou eaten of the tree, whereof I commanded thee that thou shouldest not eat?"

And the man said, "The woman whom thou gavest to be with me, she gave me of the tree, and I did eat."

And the Lord God said unto the woman, "What is this that thou hast done?" And the woman said, "The serpent beguiled me, and I did eat."

And the Lord God said unto the serpent, "Because thou has done this, thou art cursed above all cattle, and above every beast of the field; upon thy belly shalt thou go, and dust shalt thou eat all the days of thy life.

And I will put enmity between thee and the woman, and between thy seed and her seed; it shall bruise thy head, and thou shalt bruise his heel."

Unto the woman He said, "I will greatly multiply thy sorrow and thy conception; in sorrow thou shalt bring forth children; and thy desire shall be to thy husband, and he shall rule over thee."

And unto Adam he said, "Because thou hast hearkened unto the voice of thy wife, and has eaten of the tree, of which I commanded thee, saying, Thou shalt not eat of it: cursed is the ground for thy sake; in sorrow shalt thou eat of it all the days of thy life;

Thorns also and thistles shall it bring forth to thee; and thou shalt eat the herb of the field;

In the sweat of thy face shalt thou eat bread, till thou return unto the ground; for out of it wast thou taken: for dust thou art, and unto dust shalt thou return."

And Adam called his wife's name Eve; because she was the mother of all living.

Unto Adam also and to his wife did the Lord God make coats of skins, and clothed them.

And the Lord God said, "Behold, the man is become as one of us, to know good and evil: and now, lest he put forth his hand, and take also of the tree of life, and eat, and live for ever."

Therefore the Lord God sent him forth from the garden of Eden, to till the ground from whence he was taken.

So he drove out the man; and he placed at the east of the garden of Eden Cherubims, and a flaming sword which turned every way, to keep the way of the tree of life.

The Maidens of the Corn

(Zuni)

WE ARE TOLD IN STORIES AND SONGS about the seven maidens with their magic wands and plumes. The Flute-player brought them to our ancestors. The Flute-player sang about why our ancestors should take care and nurture the gift of the seven bright maidens, corn. He advised people to nourish the gift because it would be extremely important for people.

Flute-player had left seven corn plants with seven maidens to care for them and help them grow. Our ancestors pledged to care for and cherish the maidens and the gift.

And they did. Each season our ancestors would build a bower of cedar wood that had a timber roof for the maidens. Our ancestors would light a fire before the bower and dance backwards and forwards all night. The corn maidens also danced to the music of the drum and rattles. They danced with the seven growing corn plants, waving them upwards with their magic wands and plumes. Then the first maiden would embrace the first corn plant. As she did this the fire leaped up, throwing out a yellow light. The second maiden would embrace the second corn plant and the fire would burn smokily this time. The third maiden's embrace would cause the fire to flare with a red light. The fourth maiden would embrace the next plant and the fire would throw out a white light. The fire breathed clouds of sparks with a light of many colors when the fifth maiden embraced the fifth corn plant. The fire leapt with less light than heat when the sixth maiden embraced the sixth corn plant. But when the seventh maiden embraced the seventh corn plant, the fire would blaze anew with many glowing colors.

And so the maidens danced through the night. In the morning they would go into the bower and lay down their magic wands, their plumes, and their soft shining dresses. They then mingled with the people.

After some time, this did not satisfy certain young men of the village. They heard a different sound of music coming from Thunder Mountain, which they were sure was more wonderful than the music for the corn dance. They also felt sure that the dance that went with the music surpassed the corn dance.

After listening to the young men praise the unknown music and the dance for a long time, the elders sent two messengers up into the mountains to find out about the new music and dance. They even hoped that the new and old music might combine and enhance the bower and the fire.

The messengers climbed the mountains until they heard the sound of flutes coming from a cavern: the cavern of the Rainbow. They had found Flute-player, the god of dew and dawn himself. As the music played, seven maidens with wands of cottonwood danced. From the cottonwood branches and buds flowed streamers.

"These maidens are not fertile of seed but of water to quicken the seed," said Flute-player. These seven maidens were taller than the corn maidens and lighter in color. As the Flute-player played, a drum shook the cavern and sounded like thunder. A white mist floated from the flutes.

When the messengers went back to the village they told the elders that Flute-player and his musicians would come to them and make music for the dance of the corn maidens. And they did.

The beautiful, white-clad corn maidens came out of their bower. The flute-players swayed as they made their music for the dance. It wasn't until the flute-players showed their love for the maidens that the corn maidens' own young men suddenly felt love for them also. By the end of the dance both the flute-players and the village men coveted the maidens. As the seventh maiden embraced the seventh plant, mists settled down and the maidens went into their bower. The maidens lay their magic wands and plumes on the ground along with their white robes and then they disappeared. The Flute-player and his musicians played, but the maidens did not appear from the bower.

The elders went inside and found only the wands, plumes, and robes. The maidens had left no trail. The people were fearful that their corn plants would no longer flourish without the maidens. They did not know where to search for them.

One of them said, "Our great elder brother, Eagle, is the only one able to find the maidens. None can surpass his sight. Send messengers to Eagle and entreat him to find our maidens."

Messengers went to the cavern where Eagle nested. Three eaglets hid from the men and begged, "Do not pull our feathers. If you spare our wing feathers we will reward you. We will drop our feathers down for you."

When Eagle whirred into the nest the messengers begged him, "We have come to beg you to search for our seven lovely maidens. They have disappeared and our corn plants need them."

"I will search for them as you have asked," replied Eagle. "I will find them. Nothing will be able to hide from my eyes." He rose into the air and began his soaring, swooping search.

Eagle traveled in the four directions, but his search was useless. He returned to the cavern and told the messengers to go to his younger brother, Falcon. "Ask Falcon to search for the maidens. He flies nearer to the ground. Since Falcon flies at sunrise he may find your maidens."

The messengers went to Falcon for help. When Falcon saw them he said, "If you plan to snare me with snare strings, I will fly off as swift as an arrow."

"We have no strings to snare you, oh Falcon. We came to beg you to search for our corn maidens, who have left us. Eagle searched for them with no success and he suggested you might be the one to help us."

"Ho!" said Falcon. "Eagle flies too high. When he is above the clouds how could he see the maidens? I will take on the search for you." With that, Falcon spread his wings and went skimming off the tops of the trees and bushes just as he does when he hunts field mice. Falcon searched for the maidens over a large distance without success. He flew back to the messengers, "I have not been able to find your maidens. Raven might be able to help you in your search." After he said this, Falcon flew off to search for food for himself.

The people found Raven as he was looking for food in the trash heaps. "Oh Raven, Eagle and Falcon tried to find our corn maidens for us but with no success. Falcon suggested you might help us in our search."

"I am too hungry to do your business," said Raven. "You are stingy. Your bowls of food are always empty and I never get anything."

"Poor hungry Raven. Come with us and we will feed you well," said the people.

Raven went with them. The elders offered Raven a pipe with the best of their tobacco to smoke. Raven drew in the smoke, gasped, and coughed. He had smoke inside and outside of himself. That is why to this day Raven is blue of flesh and black of dress, with tears in his eyes. The people then brought Raven the best of their corn. Raven ate the corn. He stood, ate, and watched the people out of the corners of his eyes. When he finished eating all he said was, "Ka, ka, ka, ka. Now, tell me what you want me to do for you."

The people eagerly told him, "We want you to search for our beautiful corn maidens."

Raven pondered their request. "There is only one who can find the maidens. It is Flute-player." After he said this Raven flew as fast as he could and left the village.

The ancestors knew they must ask Flute-player for his help. They started their search for him and found him beside the rubbish heap where they had first begged Raven to help them.

Flute-player was dirty, his clothes were tattered and torn, his eyes were bleary, and he acted like a rude clown. The people begged him to come with them to hear the pleas of the elders. Flute-player strutted into the group of the elders with loutish noise and roughness. The ancestors begged him to find the corn maidens and bring them back. "After all, it was you who first brought the maidens to us. You must help us," they begged.

Flute-player only insulted and laughed at the people and behaved quite badly. Then, a shaman went up to the Flute-player and put his hand between Flute-player's lips and wiped away what was on his lips.

"You have taken the breath of reversal from me," said the Flute-player. "Now, you must purify yourselves and then we will speak with dignity and pride." The god of dew and dawn stood before the elders with great presence.

The people did as Flute-player had told them. They purified themselves and chose four youths who were already pure and sinless to travel with Flute-player. They traveled to the land of summer. Flute-player made his music, and butterflies and birds came to him and fed on the mists that came from his flute. The seven maidens were in the land of summer. They came to meet Flute-player when they heard his music.

With Flute-player making his music, they all traveled back to the village. There was such a celebration when the people saw their beloved maidens again! A new bower was built and the fire was lighted. The corn maidens danced all night. They danced to the seven growing corn plants and motioned them upwards. Each maiden embraced the plant that was hers while the fire threw out its lights.

This time, in their embrace of the plants, each maiden gave each plant some essence of herself. The maidens then drew into the shadows and melted into the night. They were never seen again by people.

Flute-player told the people that from this time forth the corn would grow because of what the corn maidens had put into the plants. However, in the future, the people's own daughters should dance backwards and forwards to the music of the flute and drum and embrace the plants. All would be well for the growth of the corn plants.

And that is why the seed for corn is held as a sacred thing. That is also why the seed is planted with reverence. There it grows and becomes mature. That is why today daughters of the village dance beside the corn plants and motion them upward—upward—upward—upward!

The Fox and the Coyote
(Mexico)

THEY SAY THERE WAS A TIME when Fox and Coyote were the best of friends. During this time, Fox and Coyote were walking together on a hot dry evening. They came to a lagoon and there they saw something wonderful: the moon was reflected in the water.

Coyote said to Fox, "Dear brother, what do you see in this pool of water?"

"It's a cheese! A big cheese, dear brother!" answered Fox. "We must take it out of there. Suddenly I find I am very hungry."

"All that you say is true, but how will we get it out of there? The cheese is in the water," answered Coyote.

"Since neither of us is especially fond of swimming in water, we must find another way," mused Fox. "I know, let's drink up the water and then we will be able to get the cheese."

The coyote looked at the water and the cheese and pondered the idea of drinking up the water. "We'll never be able to finish drinking the water. I'll make the noble sacrifice and dive for it."

Saying this, the coyote threw himself into the water and thrashed about. He could not get under the surface of the water, so in frustration he climbed out. As he shook himself he said, "Dear brother! I am not able to dive. I can't get under the water, so maybe you need to tie a stone onto me. Then I'll be able to dive and get the cheese out."

"You are right, wise Coyote," said Fox. "I'll tie this stone to you and then you can get straight to the bottom and get the cheese."

Fox carefully tied the stone to Coyote, and Coyote again dived into the water. Bubbles rose from where he had gone under the water. Then after a while the bubbles stopped. Coyote had gone straight to the bottom and died. He never came out.

Fox didn't know that Coyote had a brother who had followed them to the lagoon. Coyote's brother had seen everything that had happened. "Well, it looks as if my poor brother isn't coming back," he said.

Fox looked at Coyote's brother sadly and said, "Your brother was brave. He went to the bottom of the water to get the cheese out. I will miss him."

The two of them agreed that what was done was done. They decided to travel on together. After walking for a long time, they came to some wetlands filled with reeds and rushes. As they had walked, Fox had discovered that Coyote was not nearly the good companion that his brother had been. Fox got an idea about how to get rid of Coyote. "You stay here, because we are going to have a fiesta in the place. I'm going to bring the fireworks and many hens for you to eat. I'll make sure I bring the biggest, fattest hens there are. When you hear the bangings and boomings of the fireworks, you must begin to dance. First, though, it is custom that you tie something over your eyes. That will protect your eyes from the smoke from the powder in the fireworks."

Coyote agreed to this plan, especially the part about the chickens. Fox went behind the reeds and set them on fire. When they were burning, they crackled like firecrackers. Coyote took pleasure in hearing the noise of the firecrackers and said to himself, "Now my good friend Fox will be coming with those tasty hens. I plan to eat as many as I can until my stomach knows that it is full."

Coyote danced with the covering over his eyes and he heard the noise of the fireworks coming closer to him. Then the fire reached him. Coyote uncovered his eyes and jumped out of the fire as well as he could and went to look for Fox. He found Fox leaning against a high wall. It looked as if he were supporting the thick wall.

"You did not come to me with chickens! You left me for the fire! Now I will surely eat you," growled Coyote.

"Don't eat me," said Fox. "Look! You can see that I am holding up the sky so that it will not fall down on us. If I let go, it will come down and kill us. I will go get the hens if you stay here in my place and support the sky."

Coyote traded places with Fox and leaned against the thick, high wall so the sky would not fall down. He stayed like that for a long time. "Fox is not coming back," he thought. Coyote let go of the wall and went off to look for Fox. He found Fox inside a cage.

"What are you doing here?" the coyote asked the fox.

"What luck, Coyote. They have put me in this cage because they are going to bring the hens in here to me," said Fox. "If you want to share the hens with me, open the door so that you can come inside. What a fine feast of hens we will have!"

Coyote opened the door and Fox leaped out and closed the cage door. The people were boiling water in a pot to pour on Fox and scald him. Coyote saw the people bringing the pots of hot water and said, "Here come the people with the hens. At last I am going to get my meal of tasty chickens."

When the people saw Coyote in the cage instead of Fox, they threw the water on the poor coyote. To this time Fox is still free. That is why Fox and Coyote are not friends.

The Origin of Maize
(Mexico)

An old couple knew that it never got so bad that it couldn't get worse. They had no children and life was hard for them. Every day the woman went to the stream with buckets to carry water up to their home. She was old and this was hard work for her, but it had to be done.

One day, she saw an egg in the water when she was at the stream. She hurried back home and told her husband, "Today is different! Today I have good luck!"

"What is this good luck?" asked her husband.

"There is an egg in the water. Come with me and help me get it out," she said.

When they got to the stream, the old man was astonished. It was just as his wife said. There was an egg. "How are we going to get the egg out of there?" he asked his wife.

"I know. Let's use a fish net and scoop it out," said the old woman. She tried to scoop the egg up in the net but was not able to reach it. Actually, the egg was not in the water but was sitting on a large rock in the stream. What she saw was the reflection of the egg in the water.

"You have been tricked," said the old man. "The egg is on the rock over there." The man climbed up and got the egg.

"I have really had good luck today," the old woman said.

"Give it to me so I can take care of it." She carefully took the egg and put it in with her clothing.

Seven days later the old man and the old woman heard a child crying. It sounded like it was in their house. They looked around and then, following the sounds of the cries, they found a tiny child in the clothing. Its hair was golden and soft like the silk of maize. "What did I tell you?" bragged the old woman. "I really have had good luck!"

"We have both had good luck," said the old man. "We will raise him as our own."

The child, a boy, grew until after seven days he was already quite tall and could walk and even talk. The old woman picked up the buckets to get water one morning, then looked at their son and said, "My son, go fetch the water for me."

The boy went to the stream. When he lowered the bucket in the water the little minnows made fun of him. "Ha, ha, boy! You are really only an egg that was taken off the rock in the stream," said one of the minnows.

"Don't make fun of me," said the boy. When he got home he told the old woman, "The minnows made jokes about me."

"Don't worry about what they said," said the old woman.

"Yes, but it makes me very angry and hurt that they throw insults at me," the boy said.

The next morning, the old woman asked the boy to fetch her some water again. "I am not going," he told her. "The minnows make fun of me."

The old woman was firm and ordered him, "Go and fetch me some water!"

Sure enough, when the boy got to the shore of the stream, the minnows started teasing him. "Look, here is the little egg that was in the water."

When he got back home, the boy told the old woman, "Make me a fishhook. I am going to teach those minnows a lesson for making fun of me."

The next time he went to get water he took his fishhook. "Now you will pay for making fun of me." As he caught the minnows he put them in a sombrero. He hurried back to the house with them. "Look! I told you I would make the minnows pay for teasing me."

Instead of being pleased, the old woman told him, "Why do you fool around? You must take them back and put them back into the water."

He returned to the stream, but before he put them back into the water he warned them, "Don't make fun of me anymore. From this time on people will catch you and eat you."

A few days later, the boy went to the cornfield with the old man and woman. When they got there the thrushes called out to the boy, "You are just a little egg. You are a little egg."

"The thrushes are mocking me," he told the old woman.

"Don't let it worry you," she answered.

"But I don't like to be made fun of," the boy said. That night he asked the old man to make him a bow and arrow. The next day, the boy mistook the chickens of the old man and woman for thrushes and killed many of them. When the old woman saw what he had done she scolded him, "Now you will have to revive all of those chickens."

"But I killed them because they mocked me," the boy replied. But he revived them and told them never to mock him again and threw them up into a tree.

That is the way things went on. The boy kept doing bad things until the old woman told her husband, "He is so naughty. He does not listen. I think we will have to eat our son."

They made the boy climb up into a tree that bats used. He knew they were going to kill him. He told a bat all of his troubles and what the old man and woman were going to do to him. "When the old man climbs up here to get me, cut his throat," he instructed the bat. Then the boy climbed up on the ridge of the roof.

Sure enough, when the old man thought the boy was asleep he climbed up the tree and the bat came down and cut his throat. The old woman heard something drip, drip, drip, down. She went out and tasted some of the blood and said, "This blood doesn't taste good." She called out to the old man but there was no answer. "I know what you are doing. You are up there eating the flesh of the boy—the good part. Don't be stingy. I am down here tasting something that is no good. Bring him down so we can eat together." She finally saw that the old man wasn't moving, so she climbed up and found him dead.

The boy swiftly climbed down from the roof and ran away. "I am going to eat you," she called out to him and followed him.

"Let me alone," he yelled back to her. "I am strong and could destroy you. I am the one who is going to give food to all mankind." He climbed a tree to hide. Shortly, he saw the ground all around him was burning. "Don't eat me," he called down. "If you try to do it you will be burned." He quickly escaped through the flames.

The old woman did not see him escape, and she stayed below the tree until the flames swept up around her and burned her to death.

The boy continued on his way. He came to the shore of the ocean and began to beat his drum. Hurricane heard him and wondered, "Who is drumming there?" Hurricane sent a man to find out: "Go and find out the name of the person who is drumming."

When the man came up to the boy he asked, "What is your name? I have been sent by Hurricane to find out."

"I am he who sprouts at the knees. I am he who flowers. Tell that to Hurricane," said the boy.

When the man returned to Hurricane he told him, "He did not tell me his name."

"Return to him. Tell him that he must tell you his name," ordered Hurricane.

The man returned to the boy and said, "I have come to ask you your name. You must tell me because Hurricane really wants to know."

"If you must know, my name is Homshuk. Tell Hurricane that I am the one who is shelled. I am the one who is eaten," said the boy.

The man returned to Hurricane and told him, "He told me his name is Homshuk. He is the one who sprouts at the knees and gives fruit."

"That is not his real name," said Hurricane.

Meanwhile the boy told a tarantula, "Build me a house. It is going to rain very hard. I know that Hurricane is going to send a heavy rainstorm. I will need protection."

The tarantula cooperated and that night the rain poured down in torrents. In the morning, Hurricane sent the man back to see what had happened and there he found the boy on the shore, drumming.

A tortoise came up to the boy and asked, "What are you doing?"

"I am drumming. I want to cross the ocean. Could you take me?"

"I will do that for you," said the tortoise.

"No tricks?" asked the boy.

"Absolutely no tricks," said the tortoise.

"I want to see if you are a good swimmer. Show me," the boy ordered.

After the tortoise showed the boy that he was indeed a good swimmer, the boy climbed up on his back. After only a short distance the tortoise complained, "This won't work. My chest is being broken."

"I knew you weren't big enough to carry me. Go back to the shore." Since then this kind of tortoise has been known as broken chest.

The boy went back to his drumming until a much larger tortoise came up and asked, "What are you doing?"

Homshuk told him and then asked him, "Will you carry me to the other side of the ocean? If you do this for me, I will give you colors like no other tortoise has."

"I will carry you," said the tortoise. The boy immediately painted the tortoise, climbed on his shell, and was carried across the ocean to where Hurricane was. Ever since this, this kind of tortoise has been brightly colored.

"What are you looking for?" asked Hurricane. "Take him prisoner!" Homshuk was ordered into a jail where there were serpents. "Here! Now you will be eaten."

In the morning when Hurricane came back to the jail, the boy was sitting on a serpent. The serpents had not eaten him. In fact, the other serpents had disappeared. Homshuk had told the serpents, "I live in order to give food to mankind. Moreover, you are supposed to live in the forests and the mountains. Go!"

The next night Hurricane had the boy put in a jail with tigers. "Eat him," ordered Hurricane, but the next morning, Hurricane found the boy using the largest tiger as his chair.

"This time you will be put where there are arrows," said Hurricane. "You will be killed there."

"Don't harm me," the boy told the arrows. "Your job is to help man in hunting." All of the arrows fell to the ground and the boy gathered them into a bundle. He sat on the bundle of arrows.

The next morning Hurricane saw that the boy had not been killed. "We won't be able to kill him this way. He is an evil one. He can't be allowed to live with us."

"I am a good fellow," the boy told Hurricane. "I will be a source of food for all. You should not try to kill me."

"Well, to settle it, let's have a contest. If you win, you can live here. If you lose, you must die," Hurricane decided.

"What is this contest?" asked the boy.

"It is a test to see who can throw a stone from here to the other side of the ocean," explained Hurricane.

"I don't know how to throw stones," said the boy. "Before trying I would like to get my own stones." So the boy went into the woods and called for the woodpecker. "I am in danger. I'll be killed if you don't help me."

The woodpecker asked, "What do you want?"

"I want you to go to the other side of the ocean and when I throw a stone you must begin to peck on a tree so that Hurricane will be tricked into believing it is the sound of my stone against the tree."

The boy went back to Hurricane. The boy threw the first stone and after a little time they heard from across the ocean, tat, tat, tat. "Do you hear that? My stone made it to the other side and with so much force that it is bounding from one tree to another. Now it is your turn."

Hurricane threw his rock with all of his might but several hours went by and there was no sound. Hurricane was declared the loser. Even after the contest, Hurricane was not able to stop thinking about killing the boy. After talking it over with others, he ordered a gigantic hammock placed between two large trees on the shore of the ocean. After that was done Hurricane told the boy, "Are you staying here or are you going to cross the ocean? My family and I are going to the other side. If you care to join us, you can cross with this hammock."

The boy suspected what Hurricane planned but he said, "Very well. I will go with you."

"Climb into the hammock," said Hurricane. He commenced to swing the hammock until it was going as fast as possible. It swung far out over the ocean. Hurricane was sure that the boy had flown out of the hammock by now so he stopped swinging the hammock. Out jumped the boy.

"You are right," said the boy. "It is really a very good way to cross the ocean. I got halfway there and then realized I didn't know where you planned to go so I came back. You go first and then I will follow."

"Very well," said Hurricane. "All of us will go ahead of you." Hurricane and his family climbed into the hammock.

While they were doing that, the boy called to Gopher, "I want you to cut the roots of these trees very quickly."

Gopher started in on this job.

"Ready?" asked the boy.

"Yes," replied Hurricane and his family.

The boy began to swing the hammock and when it had reached its greatest swing, Gopher ate through the last root. The hammock and trees flew out and fell into the ocean. All of those in the hammock were killed except Hurricane. When Hurricane made it to the shore he begged the boy, "Forgive me. Now I really know who you are."

"What are you going to offer me?" asked the boy.

"I promise that when you are dry I will water your head," promised Hurricane.

Ever since then, during the dry months of June and July, Hurricane has watered the fields for Homshuk to grow so people will have corn to eat.

Food for Thought

- What are some uses of rose hips, such as those the escaping Cheyenne women in "The Wolf Helper" demonstrated? Research rose hips and find out what medicinal and nutritional uses they have.
- Make a list of other stories in which herbs and food found in nature have saved a person's life. Discuss.
- Find some rose hips in late summer or fall. Flatten them and dry these cakes as the women did in "The Wolf Helper."
- Find a piece of music that best suits the story mood, characters, or setting for one of the stories in this section. Act out a scene from the book using only the selected music—no words, only music and actions.
- Create your own music as background for one of these stories. Make your own instruments. For example, drums can be made out of old coffee cans, or create a tambourine out of two paper plates and dried beans.
- Develop story picture panels for one of the stories in this section. An animated film or slide show could be an extension of these "storyboards." In addition to displaying the storyboards, one person could act out the action of the story while another person acts as the narrator. A puppet show may serve as another extension to this activity.
- Draw a map that would accompany one of the stories in this section. Include terrain, population, and tribes on the map. Be sure to note the climate and seasons as well.

- Create your own original food legend. Be sure to include the following: time of event, purpose, similarities and relation to other holidays, religions, and/or events in history. What are the festivities surrounding the celebration? Explain in detail all of the customs (e.g., costumes, meals, dances, fasting, etc.).

- Keep a list of words that are new to you. Find out all you can about them. Get in a small group and share the words and meanings with each other. How many others had the same words on their lists? Use the new words in sentences or even create a short story using all of the new words throughout the story.

- During one of your family celebrations, such as Thanksgiving or some other holiday with a festive meal, tell a story at the table of a legend connected with one of the dishes (e.g., sweet potatoes, turkey, ham, duck, etc.). Ask others what stories or legends they have heard that revolve around food. Create a new tradition for your family to observe every year.

- Observe your relatives at a family gathering. Describe in fancy, humor, or fact how people eat. What seem to be their favorite dishes? Discuss what specific foods are relevant to a particular person's life. Do certain foods create a strong memory of a childhood moment or holiday?

- Create a melody and rhythm to accompany one of the stories. Share it with others. Using homemade instruments, play the melody in the background while others act out a scene from a story. Concentrate on enhancing the mood of the scene and the vocal tones of the narrator.

- Have a picnic outside and pay close attention to the surrounding environment. Are there any ideal spots for shelter? Are there other sources of food (besides your picnic lunch)? What would you do for water? Discuss.

- What personal stories do you have about animals coming to either another animal's or a person's rescue? What type of relationship did the two parties have? Were they natural enemies or allies?

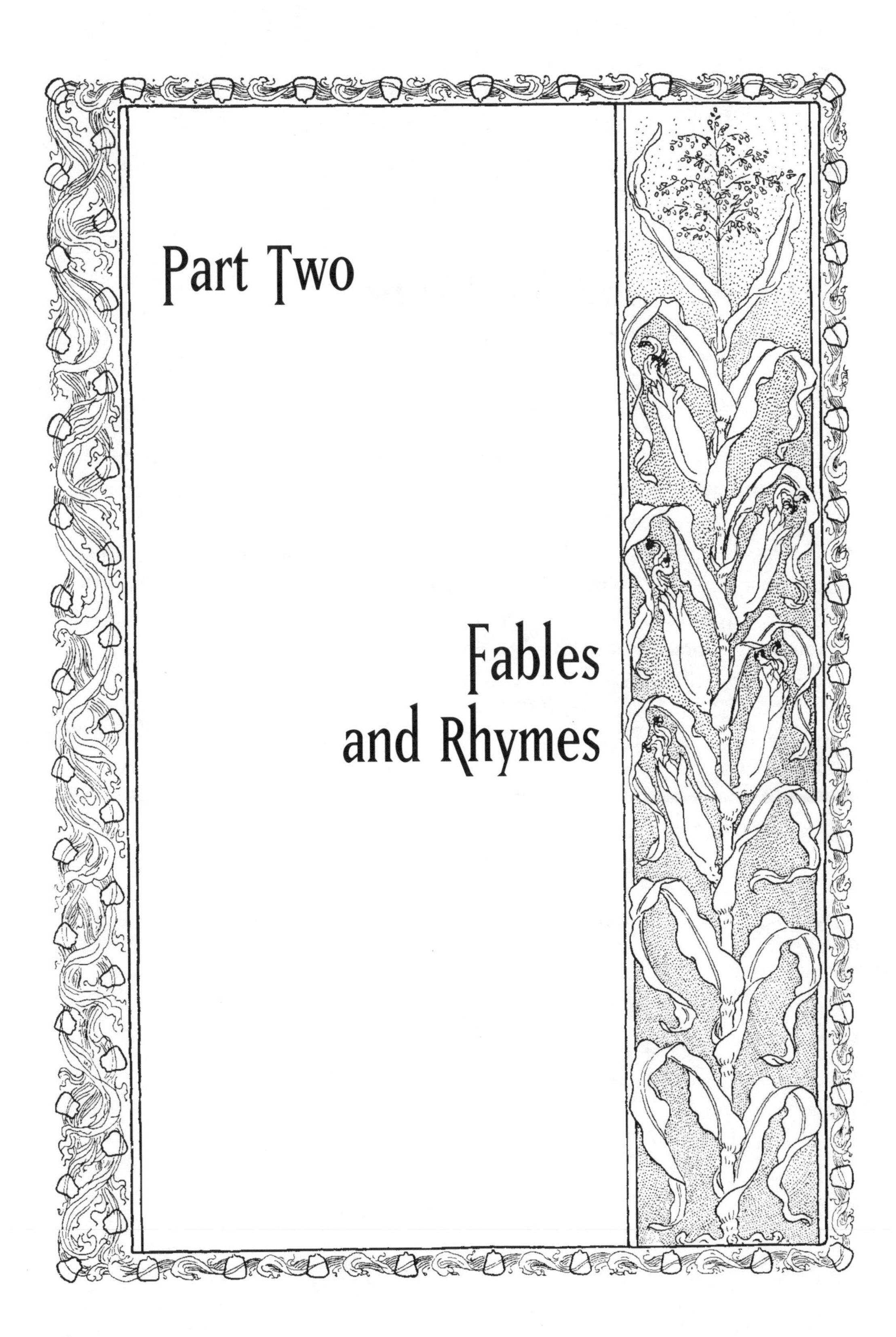

Part Two

Fables and Rhymes

The Fox and the Grapes

(Aesop of Ancient Greece)

ONE HOT SUMMER'S DAY a fox was strolling through an orchard till he came to a bunch of grapes just ripening on a vine that had been trained over a lofty branch. "Just the thing to quench my thirst," quoth he. Drawing back a few paces, he took a run and a jump, and just missed the bunch. Turning around again with a one, two, three, he jumped up, but with no greater success. Again and again he tried for the tempting morsel, but at last had to give it up, and walked away with his nose in the air, saying, "I am sure they are sour."

The Goose with the Golden Eggs

(Aesop of Ancient Greece)

ONE DAY A COUNTRYMAN going to the nest of his goose found there an egg all yellow and glittering. When he took it up it was as heavy as lead and he was going to throw it away, because he thought a trick had been played upon him. But he took it home on second thought, and soon found to his delight that it was an egg of pure gold. Every morning the same thing occurred, and he soon became rich by selling his eggs. As he grew rich he grew greedy, and thinking to get at once all the gold the goose could give, he killed it and opened it only to find—nothing!

The Little Red Hen
(United States)

Little Red Hen lived in the barnyard with her three little chicks and her friends the cat, the dog, the pig, and the duck. One morning while she was pecking around on the ground she found some grains of wheat. She went to her friends and asked, "Who will help me plant these seeds?"

"Not I," said the cat.

"Not I," said the dog.

"Not I," said the pig.

"Not I," said the duck.

"Then I will do it myself," said Little Red Hen. And she did. The grains of wheat sprouted and grew into tall ripe stalks of wheat. She went to her friends and asked, "Who will help me cut these stalks of wheat?"

"Not I," said the cat.

"Not I," said the dog.

"Not I," said the pig.

"Not I," said the duck.

"Then I will do it myself," said Little Red Hen. And she did. Next, Little Red Hen went to her friends and asked, "Who will help me thresh this wheat?"

"Not I," said the cat.

"Not I," said the dog.

"Not I," said the pig.

"Not I," said the duck.

"Then I will do it myself," said Little Red Hen. And she did. Next, Little Red Hen went to her friends and asked, "Who will help me grind these grains of wheat into flour?"

"Not I," said the cat.

"Not I," said the dog.

"Not I," said the pig.

"Not I," said the duck.

"Then I will do it myself," said Little Red Hen. And she did. Next, Little Red Hen went to her friends and asked, "Who will help me bake this flour into bread?"

"Not I," said the cat.

"Not I," said the dog.

"Not I," said the pig.

"Not I," said the duck.

"Then I will do it myself," said Little Red Hen. And she did. After the bread was baked and out of the oven Little Red Hen called to her friends and asked, "Who will help me eat this bread?"

"I will," said the cat.

"I will," said the dog.

"I will," said the pig.

"I will," said the duck.

"Oh no," said Little Red Hen. "My chicks and I will eat the bread." And they did.

The Modern Little Red Hen*
(United States)

Once upon a time, there was a little red hen who scratched about and uncovered some grains of wheat. She called her barnyard neighbors and said,

"If we work together and plant this wheat, we will have some fine bread to eat. Who will help me plant the wheat?"

"Not I," said the cow.

"Not I," said the duck.

"Not I," said the goose.

"Then I will," said the little red hen, and she did.

The wheat grew tall and ripened into golden grain. "Who will help me reap my wheat?" asked the little red hen.

"Not I," said the duck.

"Out of my classification," said the pig.

"I'd lose my seniority," said the cow.

"I'd lose my unemployment insurance," said the goose.

Then it came time to bake the bread.

"That's overtime for me," said the cow.

"I'm a dropout and never learned how," said the duck.

"I'd lose my welfare benefits," said the pig.

"If I'm the only one helping, that's discrimination," said the goose.

"Then I will," said the little red hen. And she did.

She baked five loaves of fine bread and held them all up for the neighbors to see. They all wanted some, demanded a share. But the little red hen said, "No, I can rest for a while and eat the five loaves myself."

---

* From *Nation's Business*, July 1970.

"Excess profits," cried the cow.

"Capitalistic leech," screamed the duck.

"Company fink," grunted the pig.

"Equal rights," yelled the goose. And they hurriedly painted picket signs and marched around the little red hen singing, "We shall overcome," and they did.

For when the farmer came, he said, "You must not be greedy, little red hen. Look at the oppressed cow. Look at the disadvantaged duck. Look at the less fortunate goose. You are guilty of making second-class citizens of them."

"But ... but," said the little red hen. "I earned the bread."

"Exactly," said the wise farmer. "That is the wonderful free enterprise system; anybody in the barnyard can earn as much as he wants. You should be happy to have this freedom. In other barnyards, you'd have to give all five loaves to the farmer. Here you give four loaves to your suffering neighbors." And they lived happily ever after, including the little red hen, who smiled and clucked, "I am grateful. I am grateful." But her neighbors wondered why she never baked any more bread.

(No one really knows who wrote this updated version of the well-known fable. But it has been widely reprinted and even read in stockholders' meetings.)

Mother Goose Rhymes

(England)

Old Dame Trot

OLD DAME TROT,
Some cold fish had got,
Which for pussy,
She kept in store,
When she looked there was none
The cold fish had gone,
For puss had been there before.

She went to the butcher's
To buy her some meat,
When she came back
She lay dead at her feet.

Old Mother Hubbard

Old Mother Hubbard
Went to her cupboard,
To fetch her poor dog a bone;
But when she came there
The cupboard was bare
And so the poor dog had none.

She went to the baker's
To buy him some bread;
But when she came back
The poor dog was dead.

Jack Sprat

Jack Sprat could eat no fat,
His wife could eat no lean,
And so between them both, you see,
They licked the platter clean.

Peter, Peter, Pumpkin Eater

Peter, Peter, pumpkin eater,
Had a wife and couldn't keep her;
He put her in a pumpkin shell
And there he kept her very well.

Peter Piper Picked a Peck of Pickled Peppers

Peter Piper picked a peck of pickled peppers;
A peck of pickled peppers Peter Piper picked;
If Peter Piper picked a peck of pickled peppers,
Where's the peck of pickled peppers Peter Piper picked?

Mary, Mary, Quite Contrary

Mary, Mary, quite contrary
How does your garden grow?
With silver bells and cockle shells,
And pretty maids all in a row.

Little Miss Muffet

Little Miss Muffet
Sat on a tuffet,
Eating her curds and whey;
There came a big spider,
Who sat down beside her
And frightened Miss Muffet away.

Little Jack Horner

Little Jack Horner
Sat in the corner,
Eating a Christmas pie;
He put in his thumb,
And pulled out a plum,
And said, "What a good boy am I!"

This Is the House That Jack Built

This is the house that Jack built,
This is the malt
That lay in the house that Jack built.

This is the rat,
That ate the malt
That lay in the house that Jack built.

This is the cat,
That killed the rat,
That ate the malt
That lay in the house that Jack built.

This is the dog,
That worried the cat,
That killed the rat,
That ate the malt
That lay in the house that Jack built.

This is the cow with the crumpled horn,
That tossed the dog,
That worried the cat,
That killed the rat,
That ate the malt
That lay in the house that Jack built.

This is the maiden all forlorn,
That milked the cow with the crumpled horn,
That tossed the dog,
That worried the cat,
That killed the rat,
That ate the malt
That lay in the house that Jack built.

This is the man all tattered and torn,
That kissed the maiden all forlorn,
That milked the cow with the crumpled horn,
That tossed the dog,

That worried the cat,
That killed the rat,
That ate the malt
That lay in the house that Jack built.

This is the priest all shaven and shorn,
That married the man all tattered and torn,
That kissed the maiden all forlorn,
That milked the cow with the crumpled horn,
That tossed the dog,
That worried the cat,
That killed the rat,
That ate the malt
That lay in the house that Jack built.

This is the cock that crowed in the morn,
That waked the priest all shaven and shorn,
That married the man all tattered and torn,
That kissed the maiden all forlorn,
That milked the cow with the crumpled horn,
That tossed the dog,
That worried the cat,
That killed the rat,
That ate the malt
That lay in the house that Jack built.

This is the farmer sowing his corn,
That kept the cock that crowed in the morn,
That waked the priest all shaven and shorn,
That married the man all tattered and torn,
That kissed the maiden all forlorn,
That milked the cow with the crumpled horn,
That tossed the dog,
That worried the cat,
That killed the rat,
That ate the malt
That lay in the house that Jack built.

Handy Spandy, Jack-a-Dandy

Handy spandy, Jack-a-Dandy,
Loves plum cake and sugar candy;
He bought some at a grocer's shop,
And out he came, hop, hop, hop, hop.

Harvest Song

Wine and cakes for gentlemen,
Hay and corn for horses,
A cup of ale for good old wives,
And kisses for young lasses.

Boys and Girls

What are little boys made of?
What are little boys made of?
Frogs and snails
And puppy-dogs' tails,
That's what little boys are made of.

What are little girls made of?
What are little girls made of?
Sugar and spice
And all that's nice,
That's what little girls are made of.

Parsley, Sage, Rosemary, and Thyme
(England)

CAN YOU MAKE ME A CAMBRIC SHIRT,
Parsley, sage, rosemary, and thyme,
Without any seam or needlework?
And you shall be a true lover of mine.

Can you wash it in yonder well,
Parsley, sage, rosemary, and thyme,
Where never sprung water, nor rain ever fell?
And you shall be a true lover of mine.

Can you dry it on yonder thorn,
Parsley, sage, rosemary, and thyme,
Which never bore blossom since Adam was born?
And you shall be a true lover of mine.

Now you've asked me questions three,
Parsley, sage, rosemary, and thyme,
I hope you'll answer as many for me,
And you shall be a true lover of mine.

Can you find me an acre of land,
Parsley, sage, rosemary, and thyme,
Between the salt water and the sea sand?
And you shall be a true lover of mine.

Can you plough it with a ram's horn,
Parsley, sage, rosemary, and thyme,

And sow it all over with one peppercorn?
And you shall be a true lover of mine.

Can you reap it with a sickle of leather,
Parsley, sage, rosemary, and thyme,
And bind it up with a peacock's feather?
And you shall be a true lover of mine.

When you have done and finished your work,
Parsley, sage, rosemary, and thyme,
Then come to me for your cambric shirt,
And you shall be a true lover of mine.

Riddle

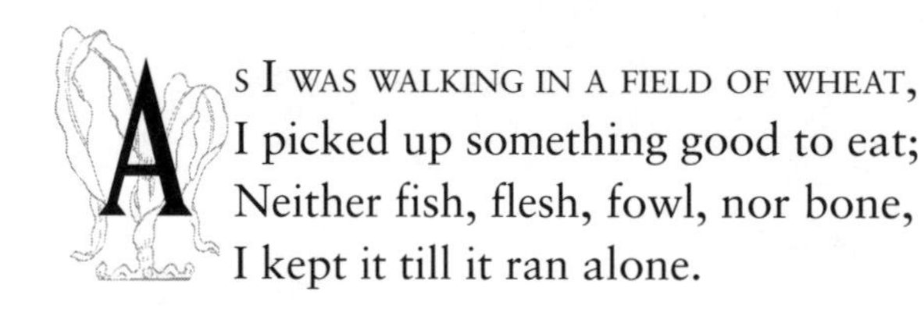

As I was walking in a field of wheat,
I picked up something good to eat;
Neither fish, flesh, fowl, nor bone,
I kept it till it ran alone.

(Solution: an egg.)

Food for Thought

- ▲ Mix and match characters, settings, and events to create a new story or rhyme. Present the new story to an audience. Go back and forth between the old and new stories to show the differences in style and content.
- ▲ Create bumper sticker slogans to accompany a fable or rhyme. Design the bumper stickers to be advertisements for a restaurant. Come up with a catchy slogan.
- ▲ Make a newspaper related to fables and rhymes in this section. Use creative headlines along with articles intended for a variety of newspaper sections: news, arts and entertainment, crime, editorials, society, fashion, foods, comics, political, and environmental.
- ▲ Develop a crossword puzzle using these fables and rhymes. Duplicate it for others to work.
- ▲ There are two versions of "The Little Red Hen" in this section. Can you create a third one? First make a list comparing the two versions of the story. For your own version, alter the story by using different story elements, (e.g., setting, characters, moral of the story, location, etc.).
- ▲ Refer to "The Little Red Hen: An Old Story" in *Storybook Stew* by Suzanne I. Barchers and Peter J. Rauen (Golden, Colo.: Fulcrum, 1996).
- ▲ Rewrite one of the rhymes into a prose story. Use conversation, add details, and give the story a beginning, a middle, and an end.

- Illustrate one of the fables or rhymes in a variety of media, such as pastels, chalk, oils, clay, collage, or acrylics. Create a story using only illustrations. Break up into groups with one illustration per group. The rest of the group then puts a story line with the illustration.
- Arrange several of the rhymes for choral reading. Select an instrumental piece to accompany the choral reading. Present the choral reading with the music playing in the background.
- Develop a series of comic strips referring to the rhymes and fables. It can be a superhero adventure series, a detective story, an animal persona, etc.
- Create your own riddle about food. Break up into groups and have one person read a riddle aloud. The rest of the group must try to solve the riddle. Whoever solves the riddle first wins a prize. The prize could even be the piece of food described in the riddle.
- Replace rhyming words with new words to create a whole new meaning to one of the stories.

Part Three

Noodleheads

Stone Soup
(Ireland)

THERE WAS A POOR, HUNGRY, AND COLD TRAVELING MAN going on the road between green fields and villages. One day as he was trudging down the road all he could think of was how good a bowl of hot soup would be. He knew it would fix everything that was wrong with him at that moment.

As he was passing by a farmer's house, he got the great idea that the wife of the farmer was a soft touch. He decided to try his luck there. He went down to the shore of the river and picked up a round river stone about the size of a large apple. He went to the farmer's house, knocked on the door, and was pleased to see that his knock was answered by the wife.

"Dear woman," he said, "would you give me a pan and a small drop of clean warm water?"

The wife was as kind as he hoped she would be and so she did. He started to wash and clean the stone with great splashing and ceremony until the stone was shining clean.

The wife was curious and told him, "You have certainly done a good job of washing that stone."

"And why not, kind lady. It is my very special soup stone," he replied.

"Well, that's new to me," she answered. "How could you make soup of it?"

"Not only can I make soup with it, but it will be the best of soup," the man said as he fondly rubbed the stone.

"Mercy be to heavens! Could anyone do it?" she asked.

"There would be no trouble at all to it," he bragged. "All a person would have to do is to watch the one who knows how to make stone soup."

"Oh, my, oh, my!" she exclaimed. "I would be extremely pleased to watch you do it. There is the pot and there is the fire, and there is plenty of water," she told him as she led him into the warm kitchen.

Things were working out just as he had planned. The man put a half gallon of water in the pot and ceremoniously placed the stone in the water. The two of them stood by the bubbling pot and watched it.

"You know, kind woman," he mentioned, "a shake of salt and pepper would not do it any harm." She gave the salt and pepper to him and he made a great show of measuring out just the right amount. "Well now," he mused. "It isn't thickening as well as it should. Maybe a shake of flour would help it along."

This time the housewife added a good handful of white flour to the pot herself.

The man noticed the dog in the corner and got another idea. "That bone of a leg of mutton that you are going to throw to the dog," said he, "might help the soup."

Now, the bone that he was talking about was never intended for the dog because there was abundant meat still on it. Even though the wife was keeping it for her husband's supper, she added it to the pot.

"That's fine," he said. "That bone will make the soup much stronger." And then as if he were musing to himself, "A few potatoes would give it great texture."

No sooner had he said this than the wife got a dozen potatoes, peeled them, and added them to the soup. "These Irish potatoes will cook up fine."

"Since you are so kind, maybe a couple of big fine onions would make this soup perfection," the man suggested.

No sooner had he said this than it was done, and the soup bubbled and boiled merrily for a little bit longer than half an hour. "I think it is ready now," said the man. He took a spoon and offered it to the wife. "Maybe you should taste it."

She took the spoon with a flourish and scooped up some soup. She blew on it to cool it and then sipped it. She eagerly took another spoonful as she said, "Just another taste to make sure. The first spoonful tasted good."

"Well, how is it?" he asked.

"This is truly fine soup," she said. "I am extremely grateful to you for showing me how to make it."

"What did I tell you?" he said. "I knew that you could make the finest, richest soup with my special stone."

They sipped, slurped, and slowly enjoyed bowls of the soup. The man sat back to rest after he was full, and lit a pipe of her husband's tobacco to smoke. After the pipe was done, he resumed his travels.

The foolish woman never stopped bragging about how she could make soup with a stone. All the neighbors laughed behind her back, and I think it is safe to say that it was probably a long time before the man came back to that part of Ireland again.

The Night It Rained Bagels

(Adapted Russian)

THERE WERE TWO BROTHERS who lived in a small Russian village. The older brother was named Igor and the youngest one was called Boris. Igor was very clever and cunning, while Boris was good, trusting, and simple-minded.

Igor worked hard growing things in the family fields. Meanwhile Boris took care of the house, baked, and cooked their meals. They worked together in pleasant comfort. Each needed the other.

One day as Igor was out in the fields plowing new ground with his team of oxen and a plow, he dug up a pot of gold. Never before had he seen such riches! There was only one problem. He knew that Boris would never be able to keep such riches a secret. Boris would immediately tell everyone he saw about their good fortune. Igor thought, "If I bring the gold home, Boris will tell the neighbors and they will tell the master of the manor and he will promptly take it from us." There in the middle of the partly plowed field Igor thought about this problem. He sat down on the ground and ran the gold through his fingers and puzzled over what to do.

"I know what I will do!" he exclaimed to the oxen. He immediately got up, ran home for a shovel, ran back to the field, and buried the pot of gold. He marked the spot where the gold was with a rock and then he took the oxen back to their stalls.

Igor's plan was becoming clearer to him now. He went to the brook that ran through their farm and took out the net he had strung across the stream in the morning. Sure enough! There was a fish in it. He took the fish and went to his fox trap. He took the fox out of the trap and put the fish in its place. Next he took the fox to the brook and put it into the fishnet.

Igor was smiling to himself as he entered the kitchen. "Boris, make us some bagels for supper," he said.

"No one eats bagels for supper," replied Boris.

"Well, then, let's be different. We shall," announced Igor. "And after we eat the bagels for supper and it is dark we must hurry to the field where I found a pot of gold. We'll have to bring the gold home in the dark."

Boris mixed up the bagels and got a pan of water boiling to cook them in. When he had made the bagels, Igor sat down at the table and ate every bagel Boris had made. For every bagel Igor ate he put two of them in his bag.

When the bag was full, Igor told Boris, "I have had enough. I am full. I will go to the field now. Finish eating your bagels and catch up with me." Igor took up a lantern and went outside. Instead of going straight to the field, he went to the trees in the orchard. He took the bagels out of his bag and hung them on the trees and then went to the spot in the field where he had buried the pot of gold.

Boris caught up with him on the way to the field and told Igor in amazement, "Look at the trees! There are bagels growing on the trees. I have never seen bagels grow on trees. I didn't know bagels grew on trees. It would have been easier for me to pick bagels from the trees than to go through the bother of cooking them."

"You are being silly," said Igor. "Everyone knows that bagels do not grow on trees." To make further fun of his brother, Igor said, "Maybe it was the bagel cloud that just passed overhead. The bagels must have rained down from the cloud!"

Then Igor told Boris, "My fox trap is nearby. Let's go and see if I have caught any of those chicken-eating foxes."

They walked to the fox trap and Boris was full of wonder because there was a fish in the trap. "How on earth could a fish get into the trap?" puzzled Boris.

"That's easy. There are fish that walk on the ground. Didn't you know that? This is one of the biggest of them I have ever seen," said Igor.

Boris was still puzzled as he tried to think about what a fish that walked on the ground looked like. "I never knew about that," he said.

They went to the brook and Boris said, "Let's see if there is anything in the net." He reached out to where the net was pegged into the ground and pulled out the net. To his surprise there was a fox in it. "What is happening today?" Boris cried. "I have never seen a fox in a fishnet before!"

"Silly Boris," said his brother. "Haven't you ever seen water foxes before? How long have you lived here and never seen water foxes before?"

They crossed over into the field and Igor took the shovel from his backpack and dug up the pot of gold. It gleamed and glowed by the lantern light. Together they started to carry it home. They had to go past the master's house. Inside the sheep pen some sheep were bleating, "Meeee! Meeee! Meeee!"

"Oh Igor! What is that noise? I am frightened," whispered Boris.

"Run, run, run as fast as you can! The devil is whipping the master. Run fast before the devil finds us here and whips us too," urged Igor.

Boris didn't need any urging. He flew home as fast as he could. Igor was carrying the pot of gold along with him and he didn't seem to go too fast. When they got home Boris was panting in terror. Meanwhile, Igor hid the gold. "Remember," Igor told Boris, "don't say a word to anyone or we will be in trouble. Don't tell anyone! You must keep this a secret."

Boris promised, "Not me. I never will tell anyone."

"Cross your heart and hope to die?" asked Igor.

"Cross my heart and hope to die!" announced Boris.

The two brothers slept in late the next morning. Boris went to the well to get some water and met a neighbor. "Why are you so late today?" asked the neighbor and shook his head with a "tsk, tsk, tsk."

"Don't ask me. Just don't ask," replied Boris. "We were up late last night walking in the woods and fields."

"Why were you doing that?" inquired the neighbor.

Immediately Boris whispered to him, "To get the pot of gold my brother found and buried in the field. That's why. But don't tell anyone—it is a secret."

It wasn't too much longer after that when the whole village was talking about the pot of gold. By that very evening the news reached the master's ears. The master immediately sent his servant to bring Igor and Boris to him.

A short time later, when Igor and Boris were before the master, he shouted at them angrily, "How dare you think you can keep the news of the treasure of a pot of gold from me? How dare you!"

Igor answered, "What treasure, sir?"

With a red face and veins popping up in his neck, the master screamed, "Don't you lie to me. I know all about it. Now the truth. I know you found a pot of gold because your own brother told one of the neighbors about it."

"My brother Boris?" asked Igor. "You know him. That silly fellow is always full of silly tales."

"We shall see about that," cried the master. He faced Boris and demanded, "Did Igor find a pot of gold?"

"Yes, sir, indeed he did," said Boris. "Please lord, don't tell anybody. It is a secret."

"So! You went at night to get it," demanded the lord.

"Yes, we did. We did," answered Boris.

"Now we are getting somewhere. Tell me all about it. Right now!" commanded the master.

Boris shuffled his feet, looked down at the floor, and then at the master. "Well, first we walked through the orchard and there were bagels growing on the trees."

The master interrupted him, "What bagels?"

"The ones that must have rained down from the bagel cloud," said Boris.

"M-m-m-m-m," said the master as he stroked his beard.

Boris continued, "Then we found a fish in the fox trap. After that we found a fox in the fishnet. It was a water fox. Then Igor went to the spot in the field and dug up the pot of gold."

"What happened after that?" asked the master.

"That was when we went home," said Boris. "We had to go past your house and it was when the devil was whipping you. We clearly heard your cries."

"You are crazy!" cried the master.

"Oh no, sir. Don't you remember? You were squealing like a pig." Boris replied and bowed to the master.

"What a miserable story. Give that fellow a good beating and throw him out! In fact, give his brother a beating as well. That will repay them for wasting my time!" ordered the master. "Get those fools out of here!"

Boris moaned and groaned as he limped on his way home. On the other hand, Igor was grinning as he walked. He was well pleased with himself because he knew they could live in peace and plenty for the rest of their days. From that day forth, Igor always had a special affection for every bagel he ate.

Ivan and the Pike

(Russia)

In old Russia there were once three brothers. Two of them were quite wise and clever but the third, Ivan, acted like a simpleton and everyone thought of him as just that—a simpleton.

One lovely sunny day the two wise brothers planned to go to town to buy all sorts of supplies; their list was long. They said to their younger brother, Ivan, "Take care, Ivan. You must obey our wives and do as they tell you. If you can manage to do this and behave we will buy you a pair of red boots and a flowing red shirt in town."

They gave Ivan further instructions before they left. Upon their departure, Ivan immediately crawled up into the resting spot built into the large brick kitchen oven. There, he daydreamed and enjoyed the quiet. That was, until his sisters-in-law came in and started to nag, nag, nag him.

"Just what are you doing up there, simpleton! Your two brothers told you to do whatever we asked and promised to bring you gifts from town in return. But, no, you do nothing but lie on the warm cozy resting spot of the stove. You don't pay us any attention or even answer us. The very least you can do is to go and fetch some water from the waterhole."

Ivan took two pails and went to the waterhole to get the water. He lowered the buckets into the water and when he drew them out, lo and behold, there was a pike in one of the pails. Ivan said out loud, "I shall cook this pike for dinner. I will eat as much as I want and will keep the rest for another time and I will not give anything at all to my brothers' wives, for I am tired of their nagging and insults."

No one could have been more surprised than Ivan when he heard the pike speak to him in a human voice, "Ivan, do not eat me. Put me back into the water and I will see to it that you have everything you wish for the rest of your life."

Ivan asked, "What will you give me?"

"You have just to say 'By the pike's command, by my own request, I want'—and it will be done," replied the pike.

"By the pike's command, by my own request, go, pails, go home by yourselves and stand in your usual spot," said Ivan.

No sooner had he said this than the pails seemed to dance off to his home and slightly sloshed their way to their regular place. Ivan immediately put the pike back into the water.

Ivan's sisters-in-law saw this amazing thing and marveled. They whispered to each other, "Maybe Ivan is not a simpleton at all. He must really be clever and is just pretending. Otherwise, how could the pails have come home by themselves? We both saw it. How did it happen?"

Not too much later, Ivan came into the house and lay down in the resting spot of the stove. The sisters-in-law came over to him and demanded, "Ivan! There you go again, lazy fellow. You just lie there and do nothing. We have no wood. Go and get some so we can cook the dinner and warm up our hut."

Ivan climbed down out of his cozy spot, took two axes, went to the sled, and climbed in, but did not harness the horses to it. "By the pike's command, by my own request, go into the woods, sled!"

The sled took off as though someone were driving it with three of the strongest horses in the land. The sled ran roughshod into everything and over everything that stood in its way, no matter if they were people, animals, huts, everything that stood in its way. No one was able to stop it. The sled went through the town and entered the woods, where it stopped. Ivan got off, sat down on the ground, and ordered, "Axes, cut wood and see that it is all the same size and cut well for the stove. When you have cut the wood, stack it on the sled."

Whippity whap! The wood was chopped and set evenly on the sled. Ivan sat on top of the wood and the sled again rode swiftly through the town. Again, it crashed into everything that was in its way. This time, though, the people were ready for Ivan and the sled. They banded together and caught him and began to shake and beat him. Ivan just took up a stick and ordered it to take care of the mob.

The stout stick jumped up and set about hitting out to the left and to the right until it had beaten and hit many people. The people were left lying in moaning heaps along the road. Ivan continued home, stacked the wood from the sled in the wood pile, and went to his resting place on the stove to sleep.

The people of the town were furious at what Ivan had done, so they went to the Czar with a petition that demanded that Ivan be banished from the kingdom. Everyone knew Ivan had to have magical powers helping him. How else could the things that happened come about? The wisest of the people advised the Czar that the best way to get Ivan to come to the palace would be to promise him red boots and a flowing red shirt.

The Czar sent messengers to Ivan's hut. The message from the Czar said, "The Czar requests your presence in the palace and promises to give you red boots and a flowing red shirt for your trouble."

Ivan, still sitting on the stove, said, "Stove, by the pike's command, by my own request, go to the Czar's palace."

The stove just lifted itself up, left the hut, and arrived at the Czar's palace with Ivan still sitting in the resting place. The Czar wanted to put Ivan to death, but the Czar's young daughter became very curious about Ivan and begged her father to spare him. Instead she said, "Let me marry Ivan."

Nothing the Czar could say would change her mind. After hours of tears and declarations of love from Ivan and the Czar's daughter, the Czar finally gave his consent to their wedding. "Even though I am increasingly more angry with you, my Daughter, I agree to the wedding."

After the wedding, the Czar had them both put into a barrel. He ordered the barrel to be sealed with pitch and thrown into the Baltic Sea.

Whether the barrel floated and sailed on the water for a short time or a long time, no one knows. Finally, though, Ivan's wife said, "I am tired. Can you arrange it that we be thrown up on the shore?"

Ivan said, "By the pike's command, by my own request, let this barrel be thrown on a shore and broken to pieces, but do not let us be hurt in any way."

With a thud and a smash-crash, they were on the beach. They climbed out of the broken barrel. As they stood there on the beach, Ivan's wife asked him if he could build some shelter for them. Ivan ordered, "By the pike's command, by my own request, let a marble palace be built and let this palace be built just across the road from the Czar's palace!"

The next morning the Czar woke and saw a fabulous palace near him. He sent messengers to find out who was living in it. They returned and told him that the scrumptious palace belonged to Ivan and his wife. "I command them to appear before me," ordered the Czar.

Ivan and his wife came as ordered. They begged for his blessings, which he now gave them gladly. Ivan and his bride lived together happily in their beautiful marble palace and prospered over the years. Until the day they died, whenever Ivan or his wife needed anything, Ivan would use the magic powers of the pike. Not so strangely, Ivan and his wife never ate pike for the rest of their lives.

The Mouse, the Bird, and the Sausage
(Brothers Grimm)

ONCE, WHEN CATS WERE AFRAID OF MICE, there lived a mouse, a bird, and a sausage. They lived together and kept house in perfect peace among themselves. Together, they were very prosperous.

It was the bird's business to fly to the forest every day and bring back wood. The joy of the mouse was to draw water, make the fire, and set the table. The sausage had to do the cooking.

It seems that no one is ever content in this world. There is no happiness with what we have, we want more. One day the bird met another bird on his trips to get the wood. The bird bragged about his excellent life to the other bird. The other bird said, "You are a poor simpleton to do so much work. The other two are living an easy life at home and here you are working hard."

The little mouse made up her fire that day and drew water. She went to rest in her little room until it was time to spread the tablecloth and set the table.

The sausage stayed by the saucepans, checked to make sure that the food was well cooked, and just before supper time, the sausage stirred the broth or the stew three or four times well around himself so as to enrich and season and flavor the food.

Usually the bird came home and lay down his load. They all sat down together at the table and after a good meal they would go to bed and sleep their fill until the next morning. It really was a very pleasant and satisfying life.

But this particular day the bird came to the resolution that he would never again fetch wood for the fire. He told the mouse and the sausage, "I have been your slave long enough. We must change about and make a new arrangement."

In spite of all that the mouse and the sausage said, the bird was determined to have his own way. "The only thing for us to do is to draw lots to settle things," he said. And so they drew lots to see who would do what.

The sausage was to fetch the wood, the mouse was to cook, and the bird was to draw water, start the fire, and set the table.

The next day the sausage went away to get the wood. The bird made up the fire and the mouse put on the pot. They waited for the sausage to come back home with the wood. The sausage was gone so long that they thought something must have happened to him. The bird went part of the way to see if he could see anything of the sausage.

Not far off, the bird met a dog on the road. The dog saw the sausage as a good possible meal, so he picked the struggling sausage up and ate him. The bird lodged a complaint against the dog as a robber and killer, but it was no good. The dog declared that he had found forged letters on the sausage, so the sausage deserved to be eaten.

The bird very sadly gathered up the wood and carried it home himself. He told the mouse everything that he had seen and heard. They were both very troubled, but decided to look on the bright side of things and stay together.

The bird spread the tablecloth and set the table and the mouse prepared the food. The mouse finally got into the pot like the sausage used to do, to stir and flavor the broth. But alas, the mouse did so with fur, skin, and her very own life.

When the bird dished up the dinner, there was no cook to be seen. The bird turned over the heap of wood and looked and looked for the mouse, but the cook never appeared again. By accident the wood caught fire. The bird hurried to the well to get water to put the fire out, but he let the bucket fall in the well with himself after it. Since he could not get out of the well, the poor simpleton drowned.

The Old Woman and Her Nose
(Sweden)

In the good old days, many many thousands of years ago, you must know that this world was inhabited by various little fairies, gnomes, elves, and such-like funny little creatures. There were beasts that could talk like rational human beings, even better than most human beings can talk nowadays. In every flower there dwelt a little fairy who sang sweet songs, and in every tuft of grass little elves played to and fro. It was in this time that an old woman lived in a poor cottage on top of a hill that overlooked a village. She had been a widow for many years and her children had all moved away, so she felt sad, lonely, and dreary by herself.

The only comfort the old woman had was that this was her life—take it or leave it. The pails of water she had to carry up the hill from the well were so heavy. Her ax was blunt, dull, and rusty. Cutting a little firewood was a difficult chore. Somehow it seemed to her that the cloth she was weaving was never long enough. The condition of her life made her bitter and the complaining was constant.

One day she had gone to the well and as usual was talking to herself. "Well old lady, here you go again. Get ready to carry this heavy bucket back up the hill to the cottage." She let the bucket down into the well and when she pulled it back up, she found a small pike in it. "Well, at last, something that is good has happened," she said. "I don't get fish this easily every day." Now she would have something different to eat at supper.

The fish she had pulled up in the bucket of water was no food. In fact it could talk. "Let me go!" said the fish.

The old woman stared at the fish. "I have never seen a fish like you! Are you so different from other fish that you are too good to be eaten?" she asked it.

The fish answered her, "Wise is the person who does not eat all she gets hold of. Let me go and you will be richly rewarded for your trouble."

"Somehow I like a fish in the bucket better than all of those swishing about free and frolicsome in the lakes," she told the fish. "Besides, what I can catch with one hand I can also carry to my mouth."

"That well may be," said the fish. "But if you do as I tell you, I will give you three wishes. That is much better than if you eat the bite-size of me."

The old woman studied the fish. "Promises are fine enough. Keeping them is another thing. I shall not believe that you can give me three wishes until I have you in the pot."

The fish snapped at her, "You should mind that tongue of yours and listen to my words. Wish for three things and then you'll see what will happen."

The old woman knew just what she wanted to wish for. "There may not be so much danger in trying to see if the fish could keep his word about the promises," she said to herself.

Then she got an idea. Just thinking about the long climb up the hill with the heavy bucket of water, she said, "I wish that my pail could go up the hill itself from the well to my house."

"So be it," said the fish.

Now that she was in the mood for wishing, the old woman thought of her dull, blunt, rusty ax. "I wish that whatever I strike should break right off."

Then she remembered that the cloth she was weaving was not long enough so she added, "I would wish that whatever I pull would become long."

"So be it," said the fish. "Now, let me back down into the well again."

The pail began to waddle up the hill by itself, so the old woman let the fish back into the well. "My goodness, I have never seen anything like that," she said. She was so pleased that she actually broke out with a grin and slapped herself across the knees.

Suddenly both of her legs broke off at the knees with a crack, crack and fell off. She was left sitting on top of the lid that covered the well. Now she began to cry. The tears rolled down her face. She grabbed her apron to blow her nose and as she tugged at her runny nose, it grew so long that it was strange to behold.

That is what the old woman got for her wishes. There she sat, and there she probably sits still on the lid of the well to this day. If you want to know what it is to have a long nose, maybe you should go there and ask the old woman, for she can surely tell you all about it!

Prudent Hans
(Brothers Grimm)

One day, Hans's mother said, "Where are you going, Hans?" Hans answered, "To Gretel's, Mother."

"Manage well, Hans."

"All right! Goodbye, Mother."

"Goodbye, Hans."

Then Hans came to Gretel's. "Good morning, Gretel."

"Good morning, Hans. What have you brought me today?"

"I have brought nothing, but I want something."

So Gretel gave Hans a needle and then he said, "Goodbye, Gretel."

Gretel said, "Goodbye, Hans."

Hans carried the needle away with him and stuck it in a hay cart that was going along. He followed it home. "Good evening, Mother."

"Good evening, Hans. Where have you been?"

"To Gretel's, Mother."

"What did you take to Gretel?"

"I took nothing, but I brought away something."

"What did Gretel give you?"

"A needle, Mother."

"What did you do with it, Hans?"

"Stuck it in the hay cart."

"That was very stupid of you, Hans. You should have stuck it in your sleeve."

"All right, Mother! I'll do better next time."

When next time came, Hans's mother said, "Where are you going, Hans?"

"To Gretel's, Mother."

"Manage well, Hans."

"All right. Goodbye, Mother."

"Goodbye, Hans."

Then Hans came to Gretel. "Good morning, Gretel."

"Good morning, Hans. What have you brought me today?"

"I've brought nothing, but I want something."

So Gretel gave Hans a knife, and then he said, "Goodbye, Gretel."

She said, "Goodbye, Hans."

Hans took the knife away with him, and stuck it in his sleeve, and went home. "Good evening, Mother."

"Good evening, Hans. Where have you been?"

"To Gretel's."

"What did you take her?"

"I took nothing, but I brought away something."

"What did Gretel give you, Hans?"

"A knife, Mother."

"What did you do with it, Hans?"

"Stuck it in my sleeve, Mother."

"That was very stupid of you, Hans. You should have put it in your pocket."

"All right, Mother! I'll do better next time."

When next time came, Hans's mother said, "Where to, Hans?"

"To Gretel's, Mother."

"Manage well, Hans."

"All right! Goodbye, Mother."

"Goodbye, Hans."

So Hans came to Gretel's. "Good morning, Gretel."

"Good morning, Hans. What have you brought me today?"

"I've brought nothing, but I want to take away something."

So Gretel gave Hans a young goat. Then he said, "Goodbye, Gretel."

She said, "Goodbye, Hans."

So Hans carried off the goat and tied its legs together and put it in his pocket. By the time he got home, it was suffocated.

"Good evening, Mother."

"Good evening, Hans. Where have you been?"

"To Gretel's, Mother."

"What did you take her, Hans?"

"I took nothing, but I brought away something."

"What did Gretel give you, Hans?"

"A goat, Mother."

"What did you do with it, Hans?"

"Put it in my pocket, Mother."

"That was very stupid of you, Hans. You should have tied a cord round its neck, and led it home."

"All right, Mother! I'll do better next time."

Then when next time came, Hans's mother said, "Where to, Hans?"

"To Gretel's, Mother."

"Manage well, Hans."

"All right! Goodbye, Mother."

"Goodbye, Hans."

Then Hans came to Gretel's. "Good morning, Gretel."

"Good morning, Hans. What have you brought me today?"

"I've brought nothing, but I want to take away something."

So Gretel gave Hans a piece of bacon. He said, "Goodbye, Gretel."

She said, "Goodbye, Hans."

Hans took the bacon, and tied a string round it and dragged it after him on his way home. The dogs came and ate it up so that when he got home he had the string in his hand, and nothing at the other end of it.

"Good evening, Mother."

"Good evening, Hans. Where have you been?"

"To Gretel's, Mother."

"What did you take her, Hans?"

"I took her nothing, but I brought away something."

"What did Gretel give you, Hans?"

"A piece of bacon, Mother."

"What did you do with it, Hans?"

"I tied a piece of string to it and led it home. The dogs ate it, Mother."

"That was very stupid of you, Hans. You ought to have carried it on your head."

"All right! I'll do better next time, Mother."

When next time came, Hans's mother asked, "Where to, Hans?"

"To Gretel's, Mother."

"Manage well, Hans."

"All right! Goodbye, Mother."

"Goodbye, Hans."

Then Hans came to Gretel's. "Good morning, Gretel."

"Good morning, Hans. What have you brought me?"

"I have brought nothing, but I want to take away something."

So Gretel gave Hans a calf.

"Goodbye, Gretel."

"Goodbye, Hans."

Hans took the calf, and set it on his head, and carried it home, and the calf scratched his face. "Good evening, Mother."

"Good evening, Hans. Where have you been?"

"To Gretel's, Mother."

"What did you take her?"

"I took nothing, but I brought away something."

"What did Gretel give you, Hans?"

"A calf, Mother."

"What did you do with the calf, Hans?"

"I carried it home on my head but it scratched my face."

"That was very stupid of you, Hans. You ought to have led home the calf, and tied it to the manger."

"All right! I'll do better next time, Mother."

When next time came, Hans's mother asked, "Where to, Hans?"

"To Gretel's, Mother."

"Manage well, Hans."

"All right, Mother! Goodbye."

"Goodbye, Hans."

Then Hans came to Gretel's. "Good morning, Gretel."

"Good morning, Hans. What have you brought me today?"

"I have brought nothing, but I want to take away something."

Then Gretel said to Hans, "You shall take away me."

Then Hans took Gretel, and tied a rope round her neck, and led her home and fastened her up to the manger and went to his mother. "Good evening, Mother."

"Good evening, Hans. Where have you been?"

"To Gretel's, Mother."

"What did you take her, Hans?"

"Nothing, Mother."

"What did Gretel give you, Hans?"

"Nothing but herself, Mother."

"Where have you left Gretel, Hans?"

"I led her home with a rope, and tied her up to the manger to eat hay, Mother."

"That was very stupid of you, Hans. You should have cast sheep's eyes at her."

"All right, mother! I'll do better next time."

Then Hans went into the stable, and taking all the eyes out of the sheep, he threw them in Gretel's face. Then Gretel was angry, and getting loose, she ran away and became the bride of another.

Food for Thought

- Invent some story openers (such as "Once upon a time there were") related to noodleheads. Collect these new story openings in a booklet. Share them. Use them as story starters for your own noodlehead story.
- After reading or hearing "Stone Soup," organize a variation on it in which everyone (in the class, club, or group) brings in a can of something. Put all of the contents of the cans in a pot and cook them. This could be part of a "Hobo Party" theme. How did the soup taste? Collect taste reactions from the participants. Ask students why they chose a particular contribution. Is it from a family recipe, or a traditional food from your culture or heritage?
- Create a noodlehead story of your own to share. Write about your own personal noodlehead story. Analyze the moral of the story. Then create storyboards to illustrate your story.
- Take some snapshots to use in a photograph album that would accompany your story. Take photographs to show the action of the story. Ask friends and family to participate in the snapshots. Create storyboards out of them for a display.
- Plan a noodlehead picnic.
- Refer to "Stone Soup" in *Storybook Stew* by Suzanne I. Barchers and Peter J. Rauen (Golden, Colo.: Fulcrum, 1996).
- There are several variants for the story "Stone Soup" listed in the bibliography. Collect some of them and compare and contrast them.

Make lists of how they are alike, how they differ, and what details can be found in some versions that are missing in others.

- ▲ Look at the weather reports for a week and make a chart of what is happening. Tell a new version of one of the noodlehead stories using details about weather to change the story. Ask a music teacher for the words to "Oh, Susannah," which has such noodlehead statements as "The sun's so hot I froze to death." Can these be used in your version of a story?
- ▲ Along with others in your group, make an audiotape of your new versions of a noodlehead story. Concentrate on tonal inflection and expression.
- ▲ Write a sequel to one of the stories in this section. One idea for a sequel to "Stone Soup" would be to have the kind wife get back at the visitor by tricking *him* instead with another batch of soup. Use your imagination for the sequel. The new story can be action-packed, a romance, or even a comedy.

Part Four

Variations on a Theme

The Gingerbread Boy

(United States)

ONCE UPON A TIME, there was a little old woman and her husband, a little old man. They lived comfortably together, but both felt lonely because they had never had a son. How could they die happily and not have a son to leave everything to? Who would mourn them when they were gone? That was the one sad part of their life.

"I know what I will do," the little old woman told the little old man. "I will bake us a lovely golden gingerbread boy."

She mixed all the ingredients with care, in fact you could even say with love. She rolled out the dough and cut out the gingerbread boy, putting raisins on him for eyes and more raisins on him for buttons. She placed him carefully on a cooking sheet and put it into the oven.

When the little old woman and the little old man could smell the luscious smells of cooking gingerbread, the little old woman thought that the gingerbread boy might be close to being done. She opened the oven door to take a peek, and before either the little old woman or the little old man knew what was happening, the gingerbread boy hopped out of the oven, ran through the kitchen to the door, and raced down the front walk.

Both the little old woman and the little old man ran as quickly as they could after the gingerbread boy, but he was too fast for them. He yelled back at them,

"Run, run as fast as you can! I ran from home. And I'll run from you, too."

And of course he was right, because the little old woman and the little old man could not begin to catch up to him.

The gingerbread boy kept running down the road and ran past three farmers who were talking by the apple tree. “There goes a tasty snack. Let’s catch him,” cried one of the farmers.

The gingerbread boy kept running and yelled back to them,

“Run, run as fast as you can! I ran from home. I ran from a little old woman. I ran from a little old man. And I’ll run from you, too.”

The gingerbread boy kept running until he ran past a pig. “That looks like something I could eat,” said the pig and he started to run after the gingerbread boy, who just yelled back to him,

“Run, run as fast as you can! I ran from home. I ran from a little old woman. I ran from a little old man. I ran from three farmers. And I’ll run from you, too.”

And the gingerbread boy did just that. He ran and ran until he ran past a goat. “Come here to me so I can eat you,” said the goat as he trotted toward the gingerbread boy, who just yelled back to him,

“Run, run as fast as you can! I ran from home. I ran from a little old woman. I ran from a little old man. I ran from three farmers. I ran from a pig. And I’ll run from you, too.”

The gingerbread boy raced on. He ran past a bear, who lumbered after him. “Come here, you good-looking piece of food,” demanded the bear, but the gingerbread boy just yelled back at him,

“Run, run as fast as you can! I ran from home. I ran from a little old woman. I ran from a little old man. I ran from three farmers. I ran from a pig. I ran from a goat. And I’ll run from you, too.”

The lumbering bear wasn’t able to keep up with the fast gingerbread boy. The racing gingerbread boy ran past a fat cat, who was getting ready to pounce on a mouse. “Here is a better meal. Come back here to me,” meowed the cat. The gingerbread boy just yelled back at the fat cat,

“Run, run as fast as you can! I ran from home. I ran from a little old woman. I ran from a little old man. I ran from three farmers. I ran from a pig. I ran from a goat. I ran from a bear. And I’ll run from you, too.”

And the gingerbread boy did just that until he ran up to a fox alongside a river. “Hi there,” greeted the fox.

“Aren’t you going to chase me?” asked the gingerbread boy.

“There is no reason I should bother myself to chase a funny-looking thing like you,” replied the fox.

The gingerbread boy saw coming down the road the little old woman, the little old man, the three farmers, the pig, the goat, the bear, and the fat cat. He turned to the fox, "Will you help me get across the river?"

"Sure," said the fox. "Climb on my tail."

So the gingerbread boy hopped on the fox's tail. He would do anything to keep from getting wet! They headed across the river and the water got swifter. "Get on my back, little gingerbread boy, or you will get swept off."

The gingerbread boy thought this was a good idea since he was getting splashed by the little waves in the water. "You better climb onto my shoulder, little gingerbread boy," said the fox. "The water is getting deeper."

The gingerbread boy got up on the fox's shoulder and the water got deeper and deeper. "Hey, little gingerbread boy. The water is getting so deep you better climb onto the tip of my nose so I can keep you out of the water."

No sooner had the gingerbread boy hopped onto the fox's nose than the fox opened his mouth wide and flipped the gingerbread boy into his mouth.

That was the end of the story of the gingerbread boy!

Johnny-cake
(England)

A LONG TIME AGO there were an old man, an old woman, and a little boy. One day the old woman said, "Before we go out to work in the garden, I am going to put a johnny-cake in the oven to bake." She looked at the little boy and told him, "You watch the johnny-cake in the oven. Don't let it burn." With that the old man and the old woman went out to the garden and started to hoe the potatoes and dig up weeds in the vegetable garden.

The little boy became distracted and forgot to watch the oven. He was surprised when he heard a noise that seemed to come from the oven. When he looked at the oven he saw the oven door suddenly pop open. The Johnny-cake jumped out and started to roll end over end toward the open door of the house.

The little boy saw where the Johnny-cake was heading and ran to shut the door, but the Johnny-cake beat him. He rolled out the door, down the steps, and out into the road. The little boy tried but he could not catch him. The little boy ran as fast as he could after the Johnny-cake, crying out to his father and mother. They heard his yelling and saw the uproar coming down the road. They dropped their hoes and joined the chase after the Johnny-cake. The Johnny-cake outran all three of them and was soon out of sight around a turn in the road. The three of them sat down on the ground to catch their breath.

The Johnny-cake kept running and he came alongside two well-diggers. They caught sight of him out of the corner of their eyes and one of them called out, "Ho! Where are you going, Johnny-cake?"

"I've outrun an old man, an old woman, and their little boy, and I can outrun you too!"

The two well-diggers threw down their picks and shovels and ran after the Johnny-cake, but they couldn't catch up with him. They sat down by the roadside to rest.

Next the Johnny-cake ran by two ditch-diggers who were busy digging a deep ditch. "Look at that Johnny-cake go! Where are you going?" they called.

"I've outrun an old man, an old woman, their little boy, two well-diggers, and I can outrun you too!"

"Well, that's to be seen," they said, threw down their spades, and ran after the Johnny-cake. The Johnny-cake was soon a long way ahead of them, so they gave up the chase and sat down to rest.

The Johnny-cake kept running until he came to a bear, who asked him where he was running. "I've outrun an old man, an old woman, their little boy, two well-diggers, two ditch-diggers, and I can outrun you too!"

"We'll see about that," growled the bear, and he lumbered along as fast as he could after the Johnny-cake. When the bear saw that he was too far behind to ever catch the Johnny-cake, he stretched himself out on a grassy spot along the roadside to rest.

On ran the Johnny-cake and soon he came upon a wolf. The wolf wondered, "Where are you going, Johnny-cake?"

The Johnny-cake only answered, "I've outrun an old man, an old woman, their little boy, two well-diggers, two ditch-diggers, a bear, and I can outrun you too!"

The wolf snarled, "Well, we will see about that," and he jumped into a gallop after the Johnny-cake. Again, the wolf saw that he had no hope of catching the Johnny-cake, so he decided to lay down to rest.

The Johnny-cake kept running down the road until he came to a fox that was resting quietly by the corner of a fence under the shade of a tree.

With a sharp voice, the fox called out, "Look what we have here. Where are you heading in such a hurry, Johnny-cake?" The fox didn't even bother to get up.

"I've outrun an old man, an old woman, their little boy, two well-diggers, two ditch-diggers, a bear, a wolf, and I can outrun you too!"

"I can't quite hear you, Johnny-cake," called out the fox. "Won't you come a little closer?" As the fox said this he turned his head just a little bit to one side.

The Johnny-cake stopped his running for the very first time since he popped out of the oven and went a little closer to the fox. "I've outrun an old man, an old woman, their little boy, two well-diggers, two ditch-diggers, a bear, a wolf, and I can outrun you too!" yelled the Johnny-cake.

"Hey, what did you say? I can't quite hear you! Won't you come a little closer?" said the fox in a soft voice. He stretched out his neck toward the Johnny-cake and put one paw behind his ear.

The Johnny-cake came up closer to the fox, leaned toward him, and screamed, "I've outrun an old man, an old woman, their little boy, two well-diggers, two ditch-diggers, a bear, a wolf, and I can outrun you too!"

"Oh, is that right? You can, can you?" barked the fox, and he snapped the Johnny-cake in his sharp white teeth and ate him up in one gobble before he licked his lips clean.

The Wee Bannock
(Scotland)

"GRANNIE, GRANNIE, come tell us the story of the wee bannock."

"Hout, childer, ye've heard it a hundred times afore. I needn't tell it over again."

"Ah, but Grannie, it's such a fine one. You must tell it. Just once."

"Well, well, if ye'll all promise to be good, I'll tell it ye again."

There lived an old man and an old woman at the side of a burn. They had two cows, five hens and a cock, a cat, and two kittens. The old man looked after the cows, and the old wife spun on the distaff. The kittens oft gripped at the old wife's spindle, as it tussled over the hearthstone. "Sho, sho," she would say, "go away" and so it tussled about.

One day after breakfast, she thought she would have a bannock. So she baked two oatmeal bannocks, and set them onto the fire to harden. After a while, the old man comes in, sits down beside the fire, and taking one of the bannocks, snaps it through the middle. When the other one sees this, it runs off as fast as it can with the old wife after it, the spindle in one hand and the distaff in the other. But the wee bannock ran away and out of sight, ran till it came to a pretty large thatched house, and ran boldly up inside to the fireside. There were three tailors sitting on a big bench. When they saw the wee bannock come in, they jumped up, and got behind the goodwife, who was carding tow by the fire. "Hout," quoth she, "be no afeard; it's but a wee bannock. Grip it, and I'll give ye a sup of milk with it." Up she gets with the tow-cards and the tailor with the goose, and the two 'prentices, the one with the big shears, and the other with the lawbrod; but the bannock dodged them, and ran round about the fire; one of the 'prentices, thinking to snap it with the shears, fell into the ashes. The tailor cast the goose, and the goodwife the tow-cards; but it wouldn't do. The bannock ran away, and ran till it came to a wee house at the roadside. In it runs, and there was a weaver sitting at the loom, and the wife winding a clue of yarn.

"Tibby," quoth he, "what's that?"

"Oh," quoth she, "it's a wee bannock."

"It's well come," quoth he, "for our porridge were but thin today. Grip it, my woman; grip it."

"Ay," quoth she; "what recks! That's a clever bannock. Catch it, Willie; catch it, man."

"Hout," quoth Willie, "cast the clue at it."

"Come away, wee bannock," quoth she; "I'll have cream and bread today." But the wee bannock dodged round about the churn, and the wife after it, and in the hurry she had near-hand overturned the churn. And before she got it set right again, the wee bannock was off and down the brae to the mill; in it ran.

The miller was sifting meal in the trough; but, looking up: "Ay," quoth he, "it's a sign of plenty when ye're running about, and nobody to look after ye. But I like a bannock and cheese. Come your way hither and I'll give ye a night's quarters." But the bannock wouldn't trust itself with the miller and his cheese. So it turned and ran its way out; but the miller didn't bash his head.

So it toddled away and ran till it came to the smithy; in it runs, and up to the anvil. The smith was making horse-nails. Quoth he: "I like a glass of good ale and a well-toasted bannock. Come your way in by here." But the bannock was frightened when it heard about the ale, and turned and was off as hard as it could run; and the smith ran after it, and cast the hammer. But it missed, and the bannock was out of sight in a crack, and ran till it came to a farmhouse with a good peat-stack at the end of it. Inside it runs to the fireside. The goodman was cloving lint, and the goodwife heckling. "O Janet," quoth he, "there's a wee bannock; I'll have the half of it."

"Well, John, I'll have the other half. Hit it over the back with the clove." But the bannock played dodgings. "Hout, tout," quoth the wife, and made the heckle flee at it. But it was too clever for her.

And off and up the burn it ran to the next house, and rolled its way to the fireside. The goodwife was stirring the soup, and the goodman plaiting sprit-binnings for the cows. "Ho, Jock," quoth the goodwife, "come here.

You're always crying about a wee bannock. Here's one. Come in, haste ye, and I'll help ye to grip it."

"Ay, Mother, where is it?"

"See there. Run over on that side."

But the bannock ran in behind the goodman's chair. Jock fell among the sprits. The goodman cast a binning, and the goodwife the spurtle. But it was too clever for Jock and her both. It was off and out of sight in a crack, and through among the whins, and down the road to the next house, and in and snug by the fireside. The folk were just sitting down to their soup, and the goodwife scraping the pot. "Look," quoth she, "there's a wee bannock come in to warm itself at our fireside."

"Shut the door," quoth the goodman, "and we'll try to get a grip of it."

When the bannock heard that, it ran out of the house and they after it with their spoons, and the goodman shied his hat. But it rolled away and ran and ran, till it came to another house; when it went in, the folk were just going to their beds. The goodman was taking off his breeches, and the goodwife raking the fire.

"What's that?" quoth he.

"Oh," quoth she, "it's a wee bannock."

Quoth he, "I could eat the half of it."

"Grip it," quoth the wife, "and I'll have a bit too."

"Cast the breeches at it!" The goodman shied his breeches, and had nearly smothered it. But it wriggled out, and ran, and the goodman after it without his breeches; there was a clean chase over the craft park and in among the whins and the goodman lost it, and had to come away, trotting home half-naked. But now it was grown dark, and the wee bannock couldn't see; but it went into the side of a big whin bush, and into a fox's hole. The fox had had no meat for two days. "O welcome, welcome," quoth the fox, and snapped it in two in the middle. And that was the end of the wee bannock.

The Dumpling
(Japan)

A LONG, LONG TIME AGO there was a funny old woman. She liked to laugh and to make dumplings of rice flour. One day, while she was making some of her special dumplings for supper, one of them accidentally fell off the table. It bounced on the earthen floor and rolled into a hole and disappeared.

The funny little woman got down on her knees and tried to reach it by putting her hand down the hole. All at once, the earth beneath her gave way and she fell in. She fell for quite a distance, but luckily was not hurt. She scrambled to her feet and brushed the dirt off her clothes.

The funny little old woman saw that she was standing on a road. In fact, the road looked just like the road in front of her house. There was enough light for her to see plenty of rice fields. The rice fields didn't have any people in them, though.

The whole happening of the funny little old woman was a mystery but it seems that the old woman had actually fallen into another country. The road she was on was hilly, so after looking for her dumpling in vain, she decided that it must have rolled farther away down the slope.

She ran down the road looking for the dumpling, calling out to it, "My dumpling, my dumpling! Where have you gone, dear dumpling of mine?"

A little farther down the road she saw a stone statue along the roadside and she asked it, "O, Lord Statue of Stone, did you see my dear dumpling?"

The stone statue answered, "Yes, I saw your dumpling rolling by me going down the road. There is a wicked Oni who lives down there and eats people, so maybe you better not go any farther."

The funny little old woman only laughed and ran on down the road. As she ran she called out, "My dumpling, my dear dumpling. Where have you gone, dear dumpling of mine?" She came to another stone statue and asked it, "O, kind Lord, did you see my dear dumpling?"

The stone statue answered her, "Yes, I saw your dumpling go rolling by a little while ago. There is a wicked Oni who lives down there and eats people, so maybe you better not go any farther."

The funny little old woman only laughed and ran on down the road. As she ran she called out, "My dumpling, my dear dumpling. Where have you gone, dear dumpling of mine?" She ran on down the road and came to a third stone statue alongside the road. "O, dear Lord Statue, did you see my dear dumpling?"

The stone statue answered her, "Don't bother talking about your dumpling just now. The Oni is coming. Crouch down here behind my sleeves and stay quiet."

In a short time the Oni came close to the statue and the crouching funny little old woman. He stopped and bowed to the statue and said, "Good day!" Now the Oni is a nasty breed of monster. It is ugly and sometimes has tusks and horns, but is also brightly colored, usually red or blue. This Oni combined all those physical features!

The statue answered the Oni with a very polite, "Good day to you, too."

Suddenly the Oni sniffed the air two or three times in a suspicious manner and cried out, "Statue, Statue, I smell a smell of a human somewhere near. Don't you?"

"Oh," said the statue, "perhaps your nose is playing tricks on you."

The Oni sniffed the air again and said, "Oh no, no! I smell the definite smell of a human being."

With all of this, the funny little old woman couldn't help herself and she started laughing. "Te, he, he!"

The Oni immediately reached his big hairy hand down behind the statue's sleeves and pulled the laughing little old woman out.

The funny little old woman was still laughing, "Te, he, he!"

"Ah ha!" cried the Oni.

The stone statue asked, "What are you going to do with that little old woman? You must not hurt her!"

"I won't," sneered the Oni, "but I will take her home with me and she will cook for us."

"Te, he, he," laughed the funny little old woman.

The stone statue thought about that and then said, "Very well. But you must really be kind to her. If you are not, I will be very angry."

The Oni promised, "I won't hurt her at all. She will have to do only a small amount of work for us each day. Goodbye."

The Oni took the funny little old woman far down the road until they came to a wide deep river. There was a boat there and the Oni put the funny little old woman in the boat. He took her across the river to his house. It was a very large house. The Oni took her at once to the kitchen and told her to cook dinner for himself and the other Oni who lived with him.

The Oni gave the funny little old woman a small wooden rice paddle and told her, "You must always put only one grain of rice into the pot and when you stir that one grain of rice in the water with this paddle, the grain will multiply until the pot is full."

The funny little old woman did just as the Oni had told her. She put just one rice grain into the pot. She began to stir it with the paddle and as she stirred, the one grain became two, then four, then eight, then sixteen, then thirty-two, then sixty-four, and so on. Every time the funny little old woman moved the paddle the rice increased in quantity. In a very short time, the pot was full.

The funny little old woman stayed in the house of the Oni for a very long time. Each day she cooked food for him and for all of his friends. The Oni kept his promise and never hurt or frightened her. Her work was certainly easy with the help of the magic paddle. Since an Oni eats much more than any human being eats, she had to cook very, very large amounts, but the paddle made it all easy.

After a while she became lonely and was always wishing to go back to her very own little house. Yes, she wanted to be in her very own house making dumplings again. One day when the Oni were all out somewhere, she decided to run away.

She had become fond of the magic paddle, so she slipped it under her girdle. Then she ran down to the river. No one saw her and the boat was there. She climbed into the boat and pushed off. Since she could row the boat very well she was soon far away from the shore. Now, the river was very wide, so she had only rowed about one-fourth of the way across when the Oni, all of them, came back to their house.

They discovered that their cook was gone and so was the magic paddle. They all ran down to the river and saw the funny little old woman rowing away in the boat as fast as she could.

No one knows why the Oni did what they did next. Maybe it was because they could not swim. Since they had no boat, they thought the only way they could catch the funny little old woman would be to drink up all of the water from the river before she made it to the other side. They knelt down and began to slurp and drink the water up as fast as they could. Before the funny little old woman had made it halfway across the river, the water had become quite low. The funny little old woman kept on rowing until the water became so shallow that the Oni stopped drinking. They began to wade across the muddy river. The funny little old woman dropped her oar, took the magic paddle from under her girdle, and shook it at the Oni. She made funny faces as she did this and the Oni all burst out laughing.

The moment they laughed, they could not help throwing up all the water they had drunk and the river became full again. The Oni could not cross and the funny little old woman got safely over to the other side and ran up the road as fast as she could go.

The funny little old woman never stopped running until she found herself at home again. After this adventure, the funny little old woman was very happy. She could make her dear dumplings whenever she pleased. Besides, she still had the magic paddle to make rice for herself. She sold her dumplings to her neighbors and in a very short time, the funny little old woman was very rich.

Food for Thought

- Read the stories in this section. Make a chart in which you compare and contrast them. Look at the themes, characters, settings, and morals. Make a list of the differences and similarities. Discuss.
- Write your own story using another variation on this theme. Give it a different setting, characters, and events.
- Check library bookshelves to see how many books contain something related to food in the title. The bibliography at the end of this book lists quite a few variants for the same stories. It may help you in your search.
- Once a review of the comparisons and contrasts has been completed, create a story of your own. Discuss how you made your story different. What were your changes?
- Visit a bookstore. Are there many books on cooking there? Were there any books that seemed special to you? Why? To narrow this activity down a bit, choose a specific item of food and then proceed with the research.
- Write a poem about one of the stories in this section.
- Refer to "Journey Cake Ho," "Gingerbread Boy," and "Strega Nona" in *Storybook Stew* by Suzanne I. Barchers and Peter J. Rauen (Golden, Colo.: Fulcrum, 1996).
- Cut pictures out of magazines or newspapers and paste them together to illustrate one of the stories.

- Smell a variety of foods. Do any of them remind you of certain experiences? Write about that experience. Why would the sense of smell be such an important part of the memory?
- Either bake or buy some gingerbread cookies. Enjoy eating them as someone reads one of the versions of "The Gingerbread Boy." Did this enhance the story experience? Are there many cookbooks for kids in the marketplace? What are some of the titles?
- When you are home in the evening, sit with a family member and share your experiences about the stories you heard/read and tell that person one of your favorite stories. Try to evoke the same feelings you experienced when reading the story. You may want to focus on one event or character to create a clear and focused account of your emotions.
- Draw a series of pictures to illustrate one of the stories. Cut them apart. (Mount them on poster board so they will last longer.) Put the sequence number on the back of each picture. Tell the story to someone, give that person your pictures (mixed up), and have that person place them in the correct order of the story. The person you are sharing this with can use the sequence numbers on the back to self-check the order. You can also create a collage that represents all the elements of the story (characters, theme, action, setting, mood, etc.).

Part Five

Herbs, Seasonings, and Spices

The Sprig of Rosemary

*(Spain)**

ONCE THERE WAS A MAN who made his daughter work very hard all day long. He sent her out into the woods one day to gather kindling, and as she was collecting leaves and twigs she happened upon a rosemary plant. She decided it would brighten up her home and pulled up a sprig of it. But the plant resisted her efforts until she used all her strength and pulled up the entire plant.

"Why did you come to steal my firewood?" asked a voice.

She turned to see a handsome young man standing by her and was so bewildered that she could only mumble a few words about her father sending her out to gather kindling.

He bade her to follow him and led her through the opening made by the uprooted rosemary plant. They traveled underground, visiting about this and that, till they came to a splendid palace. Then he hold her that he was a lord and that he would be pleased if she would marry him. Realizing that her life would be much better than her former miserable existence and that this young lord was quite congenial, she agreed to his proposal. Soon they were married.

The lord had a housekeeper who gave the girl the keys to the house, cautioning her that she was to never use one particular key to open a chest. If she did it would be the ruination of them all. The girl promised, but the presence of the key tugged at her mind. One day she could no longer resist the need to learn what was in the chest and she inserted the key and carefully lifted the lid.

---

*From *Wise Women* by Suzanne I. Barchers. Englewood, Colo.: Libraries Unlimited, 1990.

Inside she found a serpent's skin. She naturally did not know that her husband was a magician who used the skin for his sorcery. The sight of the skin made her feel ill, but before she could close the chest, the earth trembled, the palace vanished, and she found herself in the middle of a field.

By this time she had fallen deeply in love with the young lord, and she reviled herself for having been so foolish. Seeing a rosemary bush nearby, she broke off a sprig and decided she would never rest until she had found her husband, given him the sprig, and asked his forgiveness for her foolishness.

She set out, walking until she came to a small house. She asked if they could use a servant and was told she could stay with them. Her sadness became so obvious that her mistress asked her why she grieved. The girl told her what had happened and how she intended to search the world until she found her husband.

The mistress of the house said, "You must go to the sun, the moon, and the wind and ask them where he is. They go everywhere and know what is happening in the world."

The girl set out again, walking until she came to the golden castle of the sun. She knocked on the door, saying, "Oh Sun, I have come to ask for your help. Through my own foolishness I have lost my husband." And she told him her story.

The sun could not tell her where to find her husband, but he did give her a nut, telling her to open it only when she was in great need.

The girl thanked him and left, searching for the castle of the moon. When she arrived, an old woman answered her knock and the girl told her of her quest. The moon came out and listened to her story, though she had watched her at night and knew of her plight. She was also unable to tell her where to find her husband, but she gave her an almond to open when she was in great need.

The girl left in search of the wind and after much walking came to his castle. She told him her story, and the wind was sorry for her. He could not help her except to give her a walnut to use when she was in great need.

The wind had seemed to be her last chance and her disappointment overwhelmed her. She sat down and began to weep. The wind was so distressed that he told her he would set out and try to learn something that might help her. With a great bluster he departed and in the blink of an eye he was back.

"I have learned something of great importance," he announced with glee. "Your husband has been hidden in the palace of a king who intends to marry him to his ill-tempered daughter tomorrow. He is under a spell that has made him forget his past."

"Can you help me, dear Wind? Would you do all you can to delay the wedding? Then perhaps I can rescue my dear husband."

The wind whisked off to the palace, arriving much faster than the girl. He blew into the room where the tailors prepared the wedding costumes. He scattered all the laces and trims out through the windows. The tailors tried to recover them, but it was soon clear that they would have to begin again.

The king decided that his daughter would have to marry in whatever sort of dress could be pieced together, but the result was so dismal that he agreed to delay the ceremony.

Meanwhile the girl had arrived at the castle. Before knocking she cracked the nut and drew out of it the most beautiful veil ever created.

When the door was opened she asked, "Ask the princess if she would like this veil for her wedding."

Upon seeing the veil, the princess was elated because hers had been destroyed by the wind's prank. She asked how much the girl wanted for the veil and willingly paid her a handsome sum.

When the princess left, the girl cracked open the almond and drew out from it the most splendid petticoats ever seen. She knocked again, asking if the princess would like to buy her petticoats.

As soon as the princess saw the petticoats she asked what the girl wanted for them. The girl named an even more costly sum, but the princess was delighted to pay it for the petticoats.

When the princess had departed, the girl cracked open her walnut and out came a dress of great brilliance and beauty. She knocked at the door once again, inquiring as to whether the princess wished to buy this glorious dress.

The princess was thrilled with the dress, and she immediately asked the girl what her price was.

This time the girl did not ask for gold. Instead she stated that she wanted to see the groom. This did not please the princess, but she so wanted the dress that she decided it was an easy request to fulfill.

Thus the girl was led to the room where her husband was held. She found him sleeping and touched him with the sprig of rosemary she still carried. The spell was broken and he woke and recognized her. He called for the king, telling him that she was his true wife. They went back to the girl's home, where they were happy through their old age.

The Rosemary Bush
(Italy)

Once upon a time when magic was everywhere, there were a king and queen in Italy whose life was full of riches, food, and joy. The only sadness in their life was that they had no children. They had each other to love but a child of their own would have made their happiness complete. The queen was strolling in her garden one day. She was certainly able to grow things of beauty. She looked at a rosemary bush and was struck with the many seedlings growing around it. "That is a cruel sight," she said. "The common rosemary bush has all those children gathered around her while I, the queen, have no offspring to call my own."

The next thing that happened was unusual even for those times, but the queen gave birth—she gave birth, not to a baby, but to a rosemary bush! "I'll plant this bush and watch it grow," she mused as she planted it in an exquisite pot. Because she was the mother, she decided it needed milk instead of water to grow, so she poured milk in the pot.

The plant grew and thrived and was the pride of the queen. Their nephew, who was the king of Spain, came for a visit. He noticed the rosemary plant and asked, "What plant is this?"

"This will come as a surprise to you, dear Nephew," responded the queen, "but this is my daughter. I am a good mother to her too. I feed her with milk four times daily."

The young king of Spain was intrigued by the plant. There was something charming about it. When his visit was over, he decided to steal the plant—pot and all. He carried it on board his boat, along with a nanny goat he had bought to help him feed the plant. The anchors were lifted and his boat began the trip back to Spain. The king was very careful to feed the rosemary plant nanny goat milk four times a day.

When he arrived in his kingdom, he carefully carried the pot and plant into his garden, where he had the rosemary bush planted so he could watch it thrive.

The king was not only an admirer of things that were lovely, but he also was enchanted with music and dance. In fact, he played his flute every day. After the plant was placed in his garden he began to play his flute and dance through the garden. As he circled the rosemary plant, playing and dancing, a lovely young maiden emerged from the rosemary leaves and began dancing alongside him. She had long, silky, flowing hair that moved with the dance.

The king was surprised, but again, these were during the times when magic was everywhere, so he asked her, "Where are you from?"

Her voice sounded like the music of rustling leaves as she answered, "From the rosemary bush."

When they were done dancing, the maiden disappeared back into the rosemary bush. Every day after that, the young king would hurry through his official duties and business so he could spend time in the garden with his flute and the rosemary bush maiden. They would dance, talk, hold hands, and enjoy each other. This romance was progressing nicely when war was declared against the king. Before he left to go to battle he told her, "Rosemary, my dearest, do not come out of the plant while I am gone. When I come back I will play three notes on my flute and then it will be safe for you to come out to be with me."

He then called for the royal gardener and gave him instructions to feed the rosemary bush four times a day with milk. "If I find the plant withered when I return, you will be beheaded!" The gardener promised to care for the bush carefully.

The young king left for the war. With him gone, his three sisters decided to discover why their brother spent so much time playing his flute in the garden. Since they were so full of curiosity, one of them brought their brother's flute down to the garden. The oldest sister tried to play the flute and was able to draw forth one note. The middle sister took the flute and did no better—only one note. The youngest sister also sounded only one note.

Hearing the three notes, Rosemary jumped out of the bush, expecting that the king had returned to her. "Ah! Ah! Ah!" gasped each of the sisters. "Now we know why our brother spends so much time in the garden!" The next happening came about because the three sisters were not kind and understanding, but really malicious. They caught the rosemary maiden and beat her with sticks and branches until she was almost dead. Rosemary was able to escape and return to the bush and disappear.

The gardener came to give the bush its meal of milk and he found the bush partially withered. Its leaves were drooping and losing their color. "Woe is me, woe is me! I'll be beheaded for sure! What will I do when the king returns to the garden and sees the plant?" Fearing for his very life, he ran inside his home and told his wife, "Goodbye! I must leave to save my life. Make sure you feed the rosemary bush four times daily with milk." With that, he fled.

The gardener ran at first and then slowed down to a walk. He walked for a long distance, leaving the countryside behind him and ending up in a forest when the sun went down and darkness set in. He climbed a tree to spend the night because he feared wild animals. Right at midnight, the bewitching moment, a dragon-woman and a dragon-man appeared beneath his tree. The gardener's hair stood on end and chills shuddered through his body. He crouched in the crotch of a branch of the tree. He heard the fierce snorting of the two creatures below him.

"Any news?" asked the dragon-woman.

"Are you expecting there to be any?" answered the dragon-man.

"You never have anything interesting to share with me," she commented.

"Well now, as a matter of fact, I do. The king's rosemary plant has withered," snorted the dragon-man.

"Ooooh! How did that happen?"

"See, I do have some interesting news for you," he gloated. "The king went off to war and his three sisters got his flute and played it and an enchanted girl appeared out of the rosemary bush. Then the three nasty sisters all but killed her with their beatings. That's why the bush is withering away."

"How sad! Is there no way to save the bush?" she asked.

"Now that you ask, yes there is," he whispered.

"Ooooh, tell me!" she ordered.

"The way to save the bush is not something I can repeat because the trees around us have eyes and ears," he whispered. "You know that."

"Go on, you can tell me. Who would be out here listening in the middle of the forest in the dark of the night?"

"Well, maybe I will tell you the secret," he went on. "One would have to take the blood from my windpipe and the fat from the nape of your neck and boil them together in a pot, then grease the whole rosemary bush with the solution. After that is done, the bush will dry up completely, but the maiden will emerge well and healthy from her enchantment."

Up in the tree, the gardener overheard the secret. With new bravery, he waited until the dragon-man and the dragon-woman fell asleep and began snoring and snorting in their sleep. He ripped a knotty branch from the tree, jumped to the ground, and smacked each one of them on the head just as hard as he could. He then drew blood from the dragon-man's windpipe, scraped globs of fat from the dragon-woman's scruff, and ran home as fast as his shaking legs could carry him. He rushed into his house yelling for his wife to "Quick! Boil this stuff up just as fast as you can!"

After she had done this, he took the pot of stuff to the rosemary bush, which looked close to death, and painted it all over the plant, twig by twig. Slowly, the maiden emerged and just as the dragon-man had said, the bush dried up.

The relieved gardener took her by the hand and led her into his house. He had his wife put her in bed and served her a bowl of tasty hot broth.

The war ended and the king returned to his castle. The first thing he did was to get his flute and go out into the garden. From the steps to the garden he played three notes on his flute and then went over to the rosemary bush. It was all dried up. Every leaf was gone. It had died.

His mood changed from one of wanting to play music and dance to one of pure white fury. He rushed to the gardener's house roaring, "Your head will roll. You wretched man, you are about to meet your deserved end!"

"My lord, calm down and come inside my house, where you will see something wonderful that might change your mind about beheading me," pleaded the gardener.

The king went inside and was led to the bed where Rosemary was convalescing. When she looked up, her eyes were full of tears. "My love! You have come back to me! Your sisters beat me nearly to death but the gardener and his wife have saved my life and helped restore me to good health."

The king was overjoyed. He gave rewards and deep gratitude to his gardener and had nothing but contempt for his three nasty sisters. After Rosemary had recovered completely, the young king decided that they would marry. He sent a messenger to his uncle and aunt in Italy that the rosemary plant he had stolen had become a lovely young lady. He invited them to come to their wedding. The king and queen had given up all hope of ever seeing or hearing of the plant again and they had a jubilant celebration.

They set sail immediately for Spain and were met with a "Boom! Boom! Boom!" as the cannons saluted their arrival. Rosemary stood waiting for them in the harbor. The wedding took place and all of Spain rejoiced and feasted for their young king and his bride. How wonderful were the times when magic was everywhere, even in a rosemary bush!

The Basil Plant

*(Chile)**

THERE WAS ONCE A WOMAN who had three very pretty and industrious daughters. They all lived across from the king's palace, where they had a garden with the very best and finest basil plants. Now this king was accustomed to come out every day at dawn to see the daughters, for they pleased him very much. One day he called down to one of them from his balcony, "Listen, you tricky girl, how many leaves does your basil plant have?" She looked up and yelled back,

Shut your mouth, you king so sly.
How many stars are there in the sky?

The king went fuming inside, mumbling, "She'll pay for this." He hired a man and a mule and filled the saddlebags with oranges. He ordered the man to sell the fruit, being sure to go by the girls' house. Sure enough, they called him over. "Orange vendor, come back. How much are they a hundred?"

"For you, miss, I'll leave them all for a little kiss," he replied.

The oldest daughter, who had called him, was enraged and bustled into the house, slamming the door behind her. The next day the same thing happened to the second sister, who was equally enraged. "Get along, you old pig!" she yelled from the door. "Imagine offering me oranges for a kiss." She too flew into the house, all flustered and hot.

"Didn't you buy any oranges?" asked the youngest daughter.

"No, of course not. Didn't you hear what he wanted for them?"

"You mean to say you didn't kiss him?" said the youngest, infuriated.

*From *Wise Women* by Suzanne I. Barchers. Englewood, Colo.: Libraries Unlimited, 1990.

"Why, we would have had all the oranges we could have eaten. If he comes again, I'm going to go out."

As soon as the man passed again, she dashed out, calling, "Come back, Orange Man, come back."

"How could I resist a lady as lovely as you? If you'll just give me one little kiss, the oranges are yours."

"Can it be true?" she said. "Go on and unload the fruit."

When he had finished unpacking, she gave him a kiss on the lips, and away he went.

The next morning, the king got up especially early and went out on his balcony to see the girl. "How many leaves does your basil plant have?" he called merrily. She looked up and taunted back,

Shut your mouth, you king so sly,
How many stars are there in the sky?

"Shut your own mouth, you deceiving girl," laughed the king. "How many kisses did you give the old orange vendor?"

"Well, that was a nice trick," she said to herself, "but the king isn't going to win." Immediately she got herself a black costume, a little bell, and a gentle little burro. Early the next day, she rode forth, ringing the bell, "Ting-a-ling, ting-a-ling." She was dressed in the black suit and with very long fingers so as to appear especially skinny. The girl rode around to the palace gate and rang the bell, but the guards wouldn't let her through, wanting to know who on earth she was. With a long face and the very black costume, she told them she was Death come to visit the king. They promptly let her in, trembling as they opened the gates. She trotted right up to the front door. "Ting-a-ling, ting-a-ling. I've come to fetch the king."

Inside the palace, the king leaped up in his nightshirt, begging her not to carry him off. "My dear little, lovely little Death, don't, oh, please don't, not yet!"

"Ting-a-ling, ting-a-ling, I've come to take my king," and she rang the bell over and over. He begged and insisted so that she finally said in a low, howwow voice, "Under one condition will I leave you: that you give the burro three kisses on his backside." The king promptly lifted the burro's tail and kissed him three times. Then Death rode away. "Ting-a-ling, ting-a-ling, now I won't take my king."

When the king had recovered from his shock the following morning, he went out to see the girl and called down, "Listen, you deceitful creature, how many leaves does the basil plant have?" She jeered up from below,

Shut your mouth, you king so sly.
How many stars are there in the sky?

"Quiet down yourself," he shouted back. "How many kisses did you give the grimy old orange vendor?"

"You pipe down," she returned. "How many times did you kiss the burro's behind?"

The king rushed into his palace, muttering to himself. "What the devil! Now I have to call for this girl and marry her." So he commanded the mother with her three daughters to appear before him. She was greatly frightened by the summons and was sure the king was going to kill all of them. But the daughters weren't very upset. "For eating so many oranges," they laughed.

"These are your three daughters, are they not?" asked the king when the old woman appeared trembling in the throne room.

"Yes, sir, that they are."

"Well, then, I'm going to ask you for the youngest."

"But how can you, sire? I'm so very poor!" sobbed the old woman.

"That doesn't matter," answered the king. "Tomorrow will be the wedding, and don't worry about its doing you any harm."

After the ceremony, the king told his new bride emphatically to keep her nose out of the justice he meted out in his kingdom. (Don't you see how he thought she was a devilish person?) The new queen agreed to this request with the reservation that the king must promise to grant her one favor before she died, whenever she should ask him for it. Soon, petitions and complaints began to come in to the king from his people. The first case was that of a man who had ridden into town on a mare followed by a newborn colt. While he was shopping in town, another man had ridden off on a stallion followed by the first man's colt. When the owner of the colt rode out to round it up, the second man had claimed that it belonged to his horse. They had argued for a long time and finally decided to bring their case before the king.

"Let's see," said the ruler, "both of you stand over there. The one whom the colt follows will be the owner." The two men joined together and set their horses to walking, but the colt, being so young, staggered unsurely behind the stallion, whereupon the king declared in favor of the owner of the stallion. The man with the mare went to seek the queen and tell her his troubles, for she was known as a merciful person. She told him to keep mum and come back in the afternoon for further instructions.

A few days later, two more men came before the king with a complaint. One had said that whenever he stayed out in the cold, he froze. The other had mocked him and said that he dared to stay out in the coldest night. The king appointed a board of judges, who asked the man who stayed out all night what he had seen. He answered that there had been a tiny little fire above him in the hills. The judges answered that he had surely warmed himself there and thus avoided being frozen. But the two were not content and continued to squabble over this question until the king ruled the same as his judges. The loser left the court in low spirits and went straight to the queen.

"Don't worry about it," she counseled. "Tomorrow I'm going to see to it that the king learns how to dispense justice."

When the first man returned the next day for more advice, the queen told him to go and wait in a pasture where the king was going to ride by. He should go with a bag of barley and a big pot to cook it in. "Then," she continued, "when the king comes by, he's going to ask you what you are doing. You must tell him you're cooking the barley in order to sow it. When he asks you how in the world such a thing can be, you must answer, 'Your Majesty, since you say that stallions can bear colts, why can't this cooked barley grow?'"

When the king arose early the next day to set out on his trip, he ordered the queen to put on the pot for breakfast and throw plenty of wood on the fire. After waiting for a while, the king became impatient and noticed that the pot was sitting in the doorway.

"I thought I told you to be quick," he said to the queen. "How is that pot going to boil sitting in the doorway?" At that moment, one of the disputants in the second argument came in and said, "Your Majesty, you said the other man hadn't been frozen because there was a tiny fire on the hillside; then why can't your pot boil in the doorway with such a big fire in the stove?"

The king went off to the country in a very bad humor, thinking angrily about the queen, for he knew that these tricks were of her doing. Soon he and his retinue came upon the man who was cooking barley in a field alongside the road.

"Man, what are you up to there with that pot? Why on earth are you cooking barley?" asked the king.

"To sow it, sire," he answered.

"But whatever makes you think it's going to come up?"

"Why not?" answered the man. "If stallions can bear colts, why can't this barley sprout?"

The king stormed away, fuming to himself, "This is the queen's doing and I'll make her pay for it. I warned her before not to stick her nose into my affairs." When he returned to the castle at lunchtime, he said to his wife, "It's just about time to settle our accounts for all this meddling around of yours." He stamped outside and lit an enormous bonfire, but the queen said it really didn't matter to her, for we are all born to die. She was very calm at the prospect of being roasted. When the bonfire was crackling high in the air, the king took her up in his coach and said, "You must amend your ways and prepare to die."

"So be it," said she, "for I'm not afraid of death."

Arriving at the site of the burning, the royal couple got down from the coach and strolled up and down, arm in arm, until the hour came and the king beckoned to the executioner. Just as the fire was piping hot to receive the queen, she cried, "Wait, all of you!" She beckoned to the king. "Do you remember that I am entitled to ask for a favor before dying?"

"Why, yes, I do recall something like that," answered the king.

"Then come over here." As he approached, she embraced him and hugged tight. "There you are, my love."

"That's enough, enough," groaned the king, trying to pull away.

"No, this is the request," replied the queen. "If you wish to burn me, we'll burn together." Realizing that she wasn't going to loosen her grip, the king gave in, and said, "Why should the two of us fry together? In this case, I'll pardon you, but never try your tricks again. Now let's be off to the house."

"I'm at your command, my dear," answered the queen, smiling.

"From this day on," declared the king, "I'm not going to dispense any more justice. You're the one who has to do it." And that was how the queen came to be judge at the royal court.

The Chili Patch

(Mexico)

IN A TIME AND PLACE WHERE LITTLE BOYS had to work to earn their living, a little boy had his own patch of chili peppers. He was a very responsible young farmer. He took great care of them. Without them, he would go hungry.

One day one of the neighbor's rams got into the boy's chili patch. You know what rams are like and the damage they can do. The little boy called out to the ram, "Little ram, little ram, get yourself out of my small chili patch!"

To the boy's surprise the ram said, "You rude little boy. What are you thinking about? Get out of here or I'll have to kick you out!"

The boy insisted, "Little ram, little ram, get yourself out of my small chili patch!"

Again, the ram replied, "You rude little boy. What are you thinking about? Get out of here or I'll have to kick you out!"

The little boy ran up to the ram and tried to grab it around the neck and lead it out of his chili patch but the little ram didn't want to leave. He gave the little boy a kick that knocked the boy down. The poor little boy carefully pulled himself up on his feet, dusted himself off, and left the chili patch in tears. He hadn't cried like this for a long time.

As the little boy was going down the road he met a cow who asked him, "Little boy! Whatever is the matter with you that you are sobbing so?"

"The little ram in my chili patch kicked me and knocked me down," he told the cow.

"Why did he do that?" asked the cow.

"Well, I guess it is because he is in my chili patch and I want to get him out of there," said the boy.

"Enough of your tears," the cow said. "I'll go and get him out for you. Just wait here."

The cow walked right beside the chili patch and called out to the little ram, "Little ram, little ram. Get out of that chili patch right now!"

"And who will make me? Not you, you big cow with horns and a rough tongue," snapped the little ram. "If you don't get away from here I'll kick you out!"

But the cow persisted after several righteous moos. "Little ram, little ram, nasty little ram, get out of that chili patch right now."

"You big cow with horns and a rough tongue. What are you thinking about? Get out of here or I'll have to kick you out!"

This made the cow determined to get the little ram out of the chili patch, so she tried to hook him with her horns, but the little ram was too fast! He whirled around and kicked the cow out!

A little dog came along and said, "I can get that wretched ram out of the chili patch. Watch me," and he started to bark and growl. "Little ram, little ram, get out of that chili patch right now."

"What a silly dog you are. What are you thinking about? If you don't get away from here I'll kick you out!"

The dog scratched at the ground with his back feet and repeated, "You wretched ram. Get out of that chili patch right now."

"What a silly dog you are. What are you thinking about? If you don't get away from here I'll kick you out."

The dog kept insisting and he got closer and closer, so the quick little ram lowered his head, took a running start, and gored the dog and left him just as he had left the cow.

The next animal to come by was the cock. He began to crow and said, "Little ram, little ram, get out of that chili patch right now."

"You big-eared cock. What are you thinking about? Get out of here or I'll have to kick you out!"

Finally, after some bickering, the ram gored the cock and left him there with his legs kicking in the air. That little ram kept on eating in the little chili patch. The little boy was quite upset because he could see the little ram destroying his chili patch. The next animal that came was a burro. He saw the little boy crying and when the burro learned why the boy was so sad he said, "Don't worry, little boy. I'll go get the ram out."

Just like the others the burro called out, "Little ram, little ram, get out of that chili patch right now."

"You flop-eared burro. What are you thinking about? If you don't get away from here I'll kick you out."

The burro gave a loud bray and yelled, "Little ram, little ram, get out of that chili patch right now!"

"You flop-eared burro. What are you thinking about? If you don't get away from here I'll kick you out," the ram yelled.

At last the ram came up close and dug his feet in the ground and launched himself at the burro and gored him. For good luck, the ram threw the burro out of the chili patch. The little boy saw that with everything that had happened in his chili patch, it was almost all destroyed. A little ant came up to the little boy and the little boy asked him, "Little ant, little ant, if you would get the little ram out of my little chili patch for me I will give you a lot of corn and wheat."

The ant asked, "How much will you give me?"

"I'll give you a bushel of corn and a bushel of wheat," the little boy told the ant.

"That is too much," was the ant's answer.

"Well, how about half a bushel?" asked the little boy.

"That is still too much," replied the ant.

"I'll give you a kilo then," said the little boy.

"That's too much," said the ant.

"Well, what if I give you a handful?" asked the little boy.

"That will do just fine," the ant replied.

So the boy went and started grinding the corn so the little ant could carry it away easily while the little ant got the little ram out of the chili patch.

The little ant went little by little, little by little, and climbed up one of the little ram's legs. She started to climb, and climb, and climb until she reached a soft spot that didn't have much fur. She stung the little ram and the little ram jumped in the air. It leaped all around and began to scream, "I have been stung where it hurts, I have been stung where it hurts. That ant has stung me right where it hurts!"

And that is how the little boy got the little ram to leave his little chili patch.

Which Is Best—Honey, Sugar, or Salt?

(Greece)

IN A KINGDOM RULED BY A BENEVOLENT AND GRACIOUS KING, the sun shone almost daily and peace was enjoyed by all. In fact, the king had time to consider things of subtle importance instead of things of crisis. For instance, there was the day the king asked his three beautiful daughters a question.

He sent for his oldest daughter and asked her, "How much do you love me, dear Daughter?"

She thought for only a quick moment and then replied, "Well, Father, I love you like sugar." That was an easy favorite of hers since the royal cook made her special pastries and candies.

Next the king sent for his middle daughter and asked her the same question. "How much do you love me, delightful Daughter?"

Again, this daughter didn't have to think too hard before she answered, "Why, dear Father, I love you like honey." This princess was known for her sticky fingers because she seemed always to be eating tasty pastries that were made in layers with honey and nuts between.

Then, the king sent for his youngest daughter, who was secretly his favorite child. He asked her the same question. "How much do you love me, my fair child?"

This third daughter took her time, really gave the question some thought, and then finally said, "Dear Father, I love you as much as meat loves salt."

The king became furious with her answer. "Salt! Salt! You love me as much as meat loves salt? What kind of love is that?" bellowed the king. He immediately stomped to the gate of the palace and stood there looking for something. Then he saw it—a poor ragged man. The king called to the ragged man and announced, "Sir, you will be my son-in-law!"

The stunned man stammered, "My lord! Great is your name and stories of your goodness. Why is it that I, a poor man, should marry a daughter of a king?"

"Because that is my wish," declared the king. Immediately the king handed over his youngest daughter to become the wife of the poor man.

Who was this man to refuse the king? Of course, he accepted the princess. He was taken with her beauty and gentle nature. The man took her home to his mother, who was quite old, and they lived together with happiness even though in great poverty.

Some rich merchants invited the poor man to go along with them on a business trip of some distance. He decided to go with them, hoping that maybe better fortune would come to him, his mother, and his wife as a result. On the trip, the travelers passed a well. The merchants ordered the man to bring some water to them. No sooner had he begun to draw the water than a water spirit came up. All the poor man could say was "G-g-good day, friend."

"Ah ha! Because of your kind greeting I won't eat you as I have others who came to this well to draw water. Instead, here are three pomegranates. Listen to my words. Do not cut open these pieces of fruit until you are alone. Guard them well."

Being very polite, the poor man thanked the water spirit and hid the three pomegranates in his pouch. He finished drawing the water and took it to the merchants. They continued their journey.

Along the road they met a traveler going back the way they had come from. The poor man talked with the traveler for a while and then sent one of the pomegranates home to his wife and mother with the traveler. The traveler kept his promise to the poor man and delivered the pomegranate to the wife and mother. They, in turn, gave him a good hearty meal as thanks.

After the traveler had said goodbye to them and started on his way, the poor man's mother said to the princess, "Let's cut this pomegranate in half." She took up a sharp knife she used in the kitchen, cut it, and what magic! "Look, Daughter! There are no pomegranate seeds in here, but diamonds. Nothing but diamonds!" The women decided to sell the diamonds so they might build a comfortable house. Actually they were so rich now that they were able to build a house that was so beautiful that it looked like a palace. They spared nothing in the building of it. However, they thought of the pleasure of others too. They built a fountain for those who passed by to use and enjoy.

It wasn't long after that that the princess bore a son. He grew into a fine boy who was the joy of the wife and her mother-in-law. By the time the poor man returned to his village from the distant journey, the lad had become a tall, handsome young fellow.

The poor man on returning to his village went immediately to the spot where his miserable hut had been, but instead he found a magnificent house. He saw his wife sitting at the window talking with a handsome young man. This puzzled him and then his puzzlement turned to rage. He was about to attack both his wife and the youth, who the poor man thought had married his wife. After all, he had been gone many years and she may have given him up for dead. As he forcefully entered the house, his wife recognized him. She turned to the young man and said, "Son, come and kiss your father's hand. He has returned to us at last."

Immediately the poor man understood and he kissed both his wife and son. "How do you manage to be living in such a resplendent house?"

"Why," said his wife, "your own diamonds made it possible. The traveler you gave the pomegranate to left it with us and when we cut it open, there was nothing but diamonds in it."

What was amazing was that all this very long time the poor man had carried the other two pomegranates deep in his pouch, dried and forgotten. At once the poor man got his pouch and found the two pomegranates at the bottom of it. He opened one of them and out poured dazzling diamonds.

The lucky couple did not spend all this fortune on themselves. They remembered what it was like to be poor, so they gave freely to the poor and in fact, they set up a shop where anyone could come and select sweets and not pay anything for them. Some of their many acts of charity brought them to the attention of the king himself.

The king asked his vizier, "Who are this man and woman who bring some joy and happiness to the poor? Let us travel to their village and see them for ourselves."

When the king and his vizier arrived, the princess recognized her father but she did not say anything. "This evening we shall serve a very special dinner to the king and his vizier," she whispered to her husband. Thereupon she ordered the cook to prepare a number of dishes. Half of them were to be cooked without salt, and the other half would be cooked with salt.

At the grand dinner that evening, the first dishes served were those without salt. Both the king and his vizier gagged on the food. These dishes were removed and then the other dishes of food that had salt were served. The king and his vizier ate these with gusto.

"How did you like the meal?" asked the princess.

"I hate to sound ungrateful, but the first dishes had no salt and were uneatable. Food without salt is not really good."

The princess smiled. "Oh, dear Father! Do you remember many years ago when I told you I loved you like salt loves meat, you drove me away into the home of a poor man?"

What a joyous reunion, even though the king was certainly surprised and ashamed. "You were right! Salt is much better than honey and sugar!" And they all lived happily ever after.

Salt
(Russia)

One deep, dark, cold Russian night, an old grandfather sat in front of a blazing fireplace. The children asked him to tell them a story. "Are there any stories left we haven't heard?" asked the youngest granddaughter.

Grandfather stroked his white beard and looked at the children. "You have scarcely heard any of the stories because there is a story to be told about everything in the world."

The children had doubts about that. One of them went to the table, picked up the crystal saltcellar, and brought it to the grandfather. "There can't be a story about salt," said the child.

"Not true," said Grandfather. He put the tip of his finger into the saltcellar and then he touched his tongue with his finger to taste. "But of course there is a story about salt," he said.

Of course, the children clamored for him to tell the story about salt.

Once upon a time there were three brothers, whose father was a great merchant who sent his ships far over the sea, and traded here and there in countries the names of which I, being an old man, can never rightly call to mind. Well, the names of the two elder brothers do not matter, but the youngest was called Ivan the Ninny, because he was always playing and never working. If there was a silly thing to do, why, off he went and did it. And so, when the brothers grew up, the father sent the two elder ones off, each in a fine ship laden with gold and jewels, and rings and bracelets, and laces and silks, and sticks with little bits of silver hammered into their handles, and spoons with patterns of blue and red, and everything else you can think of that costs too much to buy.

But he made Ivan the Ninny stay at home, and did not give him a ship at all. Ivan saw his brothers go sailing off over the sea on a summer morning, to make their fortunes and come back rich men; then, for the first time in his life, he wanted to work and do something useful. He went to his father and kissed his hand, and he kissed the hand of his little old mother, and he begged his father to give him a ship so that he could try his fortune like his brothers.

"But you have never done a wise thing in your life, and no one could count all the silly things you've done if he spent a hundred days in counting," said his father.

"True," said Ivan. "But now I am going to be wise, and sail the sea and come back with something in my pockets to show that I am not a ninny any longer. Give me just a little ship, father mine—just a little ship for myself."

"Give him a little ship," said the mother. "He may not be a ninny after all."

"Very well," said his father. "I will give him a little ship. But I am not going to waste good money by giving him a rich cargo."

"Give me any cargo you like," said Ivan.

So his father gave him a little ship, a little old ship, and a cargo of rags and scraps and things that were not fit for anything but to be thrown away. And he gave him a crew of ancient old sailormen who were past work. Ivan went on board and sailed away at sunset, like the ninny he was. And the feeble, ancient, old sailormen pulled up the ragged dirty sails, and away they went over the sea to learn what fortune, good or bad, was about to come to a crew of old men with a ninny for a master.

The fourth day after they set sail there came a great wind over the sea. The feeble old men did the best they could with the ship. The old torn sails tore from the masts and the wind did what it pleased, and threw the little ship on an unknown island away in the middle of the sea. Then the wind dropped, and left the little ship on the beach. Ivan the Ninny and his ancient old men, like good Russians, were thankful that they were still alive.

"Well, children," said Ivan, for he knew how to talk to sailors, "you stay here and mend the sails and make new ones out of the rags we carry as cargo, while I go inland and see if there is anything that could be of use to us."

So the ancient old sailormen sat on deck with their legs crossed and made sails out of rags, of torn scraps of old brocades, of soiled embroidered shawls, of all the rubbish that they had with them for a cargo. You never saw such sails. The tide came up and floated the ship, and they threw out anchors at bow and stern, and sat there in the sunlight, making sails and patching them and talking of the days when they were young. All this while Ivan the Ninny went walking off into the island.

In the middle of that island was a high mountain, a high mountain it was, and so white that when he came near it Ivan the Ninny began thinking of sheepskin coats, although it was midsummer and the sun was hot in the sky. The trees were green round about, but there was nothing growing on the mountain at all. It was just a great white mountain piled up into the sky in the middle of a green island. Ivan walked a little way up the white slopes of the mountain, and then, because he felt thirsty, he thought he would let a little snow melt in his mouth. He took some in his fingers and stuffed it in. Quickly enough it came out again, I can tell you, for the mountain was not made of snow but of good Russian salt. And if you want to try what a mountful of salt is like, you may.

Ivan the Ninny did not stop to think twice. The salt was so clean and shone so brightly in the sunlight. He just turned round and ran back to the shore, and called out to his ancient old sailormen and told them to empty everything they had on board over into the sea. Over it all went, rags and tags and rotten timbers, till the little ship was as empty as a soup bowl after supper. And then those ancient old men were set to work carrying salt from the mountain and taking it on board the little ship, and stowing it away below deck till there was not room for another grain.

Ivan the Ninny would have liked to take the whole mountain but there was not room in the little ship. And for that the ancient old sailormen thanked heaven because their backs ached and their old legs were weak, and they said they would have died if they had had to carry any more.

Then they hoisted up the new sails they had patched together out of the rags and scraps of shawls and old brocades, and they sailed away once more over the blue sea. The wind stood fair, and they sailed before it. The ancient old sailors rested their backs, and told old tales, and took turn and turn about at the rudder.

After many days' sailing they came to a town, with towers and churches and painted roofs, all set on the side of a hill that sloped down into the sea. At the foot of the hill was a quiet harbor. They sailed in there and moored the ship and hauled down their patchwork sails.

Ivan the Ninny went ashore, and took with him a little bag of clean white salt to show what kind of goods he had for sale, and he asked his way to the palace of the Tzar of that town. He came to the palace, went in, and bowed to the ground before the Tzar.

"Who are you?" said the Tzar.

"I, great lord, am a Russian merchant. Here in a bag is some of my merchandise. I beg your leave to trade with your subjects in this town."

"Let me see what is in the bag," said the Tzar.

Ivan the Ninny took a handful from the bag and showed it to the Tzar.

"What is it?" said the Tzar.

"Good Russian salt," said Ivan the Ninny.

Now in that country they had never heard of salt, and the Tzar looked at the salt, and he looked at Ivan and he laughed.

"Why, this," said he, "is nothing but white dust and that we can pick up for nothing. The men of my town have no need to trade with you. You must be a ninny."

Ivan grew very red, for he knew what his father used to call him. He was ashamed to say anything. He bowed to the ground, and went away out of the palace.

When he was outside he thought to himself, "I wonder what sort of salt they use in these parts if they do not know good Russian salt when they see it. I will go to the kitchen."

He went round to the back door of the palace and put his head into the kitchen and said, "I am very tired. May I sit down here and rest a little while?"

"Come in," said one of the cooks. "But you must sit just there, and not put even your little finger in the way of us. We are the Tzar's cooks and we are in the middle of making ready his dinner." The cook put a stool in a corner out of the way, and Ivan slipped in round the door, and sat down in the corner and looked about him.

There were seven cooks at least, boiling and baking, and stewing and toasting, and roasting and frying. And as for scullions, they were as thick as cockroaches, dozens of them, running to and fro, tumbling over each other, and helping the cooks.

Ivan the Ninny sat on his stool, with his legs tucked under him and the bag of salt on his knees. He watched the cooks and the scullions, but he did not see them put anything in the dishes which he thought could take the place of salt. No. The meat was without salt, the kasha was without salt, and there was no salt in the potatoes. Ivan nearly turned sick at the thought of the tastelessness of all that food.

There came the moment when all the cooks and scullions ran out of the kitchen to fetch the silver platters on which to lay the dishes. Ivan slipped down from his stool, and running from stove to stove, from saucepan to frying pan, he dripped a pinch of salt, just what was wanted, no more no less, in every one of the dishes. Then he ran back to the stool in the corner, and sat there and watched the dishes being put on the silver platters and carried off in gold embroidered napkins to be the dinner of the Tzar.

The Tzar sat at the table and took his first spoonful of soup. "The soup is very good today," said he, and he finishes the soup to the last drop.

"I've never known the soup so good," said the Tzaritza, and she finishes hers.

"This is the best soup I ever tasted," said the Princess, and down goes hers and she, you know, was the prettiest princess who ever had dinner in this world.

It was the same with the kasha and the same with the meat. The Tzar and the Tzaritza and the Princess wondered why they had never had so good a dinner in all their lives before.

"Call the cooks," says the Tzar. And they called the cooks, and the cooks all came in and bowed to the ground. They stood in a row before the Tzar.

"What did you put in the dishes today that you never put before?" said the Tzar.

"We put nothing unusual, your greatness," said the cooks and bow to the ground again.

"Then why do the dishes taste better?"

"We do not know, your greatness," said the cooks.

"Call the scullions," said the Tzar. The scullions were called and they too bowed to the ground and stood in a row before the Tzar.

"What was done in the kitchen today that has not been done there before?" said the Tzar.

"Nothing, Your Greatness," said all the scullions except one.

That one scullion bowed again, and kept on bowing and then he said, "Please, Your Greatness, please, great lord, there is usually none in the kitchen but ourselves. Today there was a young Russian merchant who sat on a stool in the corner and said he was tired."

"Call the merchant," said the Tzar.

So they brought in Ivan the Ninny, and he bowed before the Tzar and stood there with his little bag of salt in his hand.

"Did you do anything to my dinner?" said the Tzar.

"I did, Your Greatness," said Ivan.

"What did you do?"

"I put a pinch of Russian salt in every dish."

"That white dust?" said the Tzar.

"Nothing but that."

"Have you got any more of it?"

"I have a little ship in the harbor laden with nothing else," said Ivan.

"It is the most wonderful dust in the world," said the Tzar. "I will buy every grain of it you have. What do you want for it?"

Ivan the Ninny scratched his head and thought. He thought that if the Tzar liked it as much as all that, it must be worth a fair price. He said, "We will put the salt into bags. For every bag of salt you must give me three bags of the same weight—one of gold, one of silver, and one of precious stones. Cheaper than that, Your Greatness, I could not possibly sell."

"Agreed," said the Tzar. "And a cheap price, too, for a dust so full of magic that it makes dull dishes tasty, and tasty dishes so good that there is no looking away from them."

So all the day long, and far into the night, the ancient old sailormen bent their backs under sacks of salt and bent them again under sacks of gold and silver and precious stones. When all the salt had been put in the Tzar's treasury—yes, with twenty soldiers guarding it with great swords shining in the moonlight—and when the little ship was loaded with riches, so that even the deck was piled high with precious stones, the ancient men lay down among the jewels and slept till morning. In the morning Ivan the Ninny went to bid goodbye to the Tzar.

"And whither shall you sail now?" asked the Tzar.

"I shall sail away to Russia in my little ship," said Ivan.

The Princess, who was very beautiful, said, "A little Russian ship?"

"Yes," said Ivan.

"I have never seen a Russian ship," said the Princess. She begs her father to let her go to the harbor with her nurses and maids, to see the little Russian ship before Ivan set sail.

She came with Ivan to the harbor, and the ancient old sailormen took them on board.

She ran all over the ship, looking now at this and now at that, and Ivan told her the names of everything—deck, mast, and rudder.

"May I see the sails?" she asked. The ancient old men hoisted the ragged sails and the wind filled the sails and tugged.

"Why doesn't the ship move when the sails are up?" asked the Princess.

"The anchor holds her," said Ivan.

"Please let me see the anchor," said the Princess.

"Haul up the anchor, my children, and show it to the Princess," said Ivan to the ancient old sailormen.

The old men hauled up the anchor and showed it to the Princess. She said it was a very good little anchor. Of course, as soon as the anchor was up, the ship began to move. One of the ancient old men bent over the tiller, and with a fair wind behind her, the little ship slipped out of the harbor and away to the blue sea.

When the Princess looked round, thinking it was time to go home, in the distance she could only see the gold towers of her father's palace, glittering like pinpoints in the sunlight. Her nurses and maids wrung their hands and made an outcry. The Princess sat down on a heap of jewels and put her handkerchief to her eyes and cried and cried and cried.

Ivan the Ninny took her hands and comforted her. He told her of the wonders of the sea that he would show her and the wonders of the land. She looked up at him while he talked and his eyes were kind. Hers were sweet. And the end of it was that they were both very well content and agreed to have a marriage feast as soon as the little ship should bring them to the home of Ivan's father.

Merry was that voyage. All day long Ivan and the Princess sat on deck and said sweet things to each other. At twilight they sang songs and drank tea and told stories. As for the nurses and maids, the Princess told them to be glad. They danced and clapped their hands and ran about the ship and teased the ancient old sailormen.

When they had been sailing many days, the Princess was looking out over the sea and she cried out to Ivan. "See, over there, far away, are two big ships with white sails, not like our sails of brocade and bits of silk."

Ivan looked, shading his eyes with his hands.

"Why, those are the ships of my elder brothers," said he. "We shall all sail home together."

He made the ancient old sailormen give a hail in their cracked old voices. The brothers heard them and came on board to greet Ivan and his bride. When they saw that she was a Tzar's daughter and that the very decks were heaped with precious stones, because there was no room below, they said one thing to Ivan and something else to each other.

To Ivan they said, "Thanks be to heaven. You have had good trading."

But to each other, "How can this be?"

"Ivan the Ninny bringing back such a cargo while we in our fine ships have only a bag or two of gold."

"And what is Ivan the Ninny doing with a princess?" said the other.

They ground their teeth and waited their time. When Ivan was alone in the twilight, they picked him up by his head and his heels and hove him overboard into the dark blue sea.

Not one of the old men had seen them and the Princess was not on deck. In the morning they said that Ivan the Ninny must have walked overboard in his sleep. They drew lots. The eldest brother took the Princess and the second brother took the little ship laden with gold and silver and precious stones.

The brothers sailed home very well content. But the Princess sat and wept all day long looking down into the blue water. The elder brother could not comfort her and the second brother did not try. The ancient old sailormen muttered in their beards and were sorry. They prayed for Ivan's soul. Although he had been a ninny, and although he had made them carry a lot of salt and other things, yet they loved him because he knew how to talk to ancient old sailormen.

But Ivan was not dead. As soon as he splashed into the water, he crammed his fur hat a little tighter on his head. He began swimming in the sea. He swam about until the sun rose and then, not far away, he saw a floating timber log. He swam to the log and got astride of it. He sat there on the log in the middle of the sea, twiddling his thumbs for want of something to do.

There was a strong current in the sea that carried him along and at last, after floating for many days without ever a bite for his teeth or a drop for his gullet, his feet touched land. Now that was at night, and he left the log and walked up out of the sea and lay down on the shore and waited for morning.

When the sun rose, he stood up. He saw that he was on a bare island. He saw nothing at all on the island except a huge house as big as a mountain. As he was looking at the house the great door creaked with a noise like that of a hurricane among the pine forests, and opened. A giant came walking out and came to the shore and stood there looking down at Ivan.

"What are you doing here, little one?" said the giant.

Ivan told him the whole story. The giant listened to the very end, pulling at his monstrous whiskers. Then he said, "Listen, little one. I know more of the story than you, for I can tell you that tomorrow morning your eldest brother is going to marry your Princess. But there is no need for you to take on about it. If you want to be there, I will carry you and set you down before the house in time for the wedding. A fine wedding it is like to be, for your father thinks well of those brothers of yours bringing back all those precious stones and silver and gold enough to buy a kingdom."

With that he picked up Ivan the Ninny and set him on his great shoulders and set off striding through the sea. He went so fast that the wind of his going blew off Ivan's hat.

"Stop a moment," shouted Ivan. "My hat has blown off."

"We can't turn back for that," said the giant. "We have already left your hat five hundred versts behind us." He rushed on, splashing through the sea. The sea was up to his armpits. He rushed on and before the sun had climbed to the top of the blue sky he was splashing up out of the sea with the water about his ankles. He lifted Ivan from his shoulders and set him on the ground.

"Now," said he. "Little man, off you run and you'll be in time for the feast. But don't you dare to boast about riding on my shoulders. If you open your mouth about that, you'll smart for it if I have to come ten thousand thousand versts."

Ivan the Ninny thanked the giant for carrying him through the sea, promised that he would not boast, and then ran off to his father's house. Long before he got there he heard the musicians in the courtyard playing as if they wanted to wear out their instruments before night.

The wedding feast had begun, and when Ivan ran in, there at the high board was sitting the Princess and beside her, his eldest brother. There were his father and mother, his second brother, and all the guests. Every one of them was as merry as could be except the Princess. She was as white as the salt he had sold to her father.

Suddenly the blood flushed into her cheeks. She saw Ivan in the doorway. Up she jumped at the high board and cried out, "There, there is my true love and not this man who sits beside me at the table."

"What is this?" said Ivan's father. In a few minutes he knew the whole story. He turned the two elder brothers out of doors, gave their ships to Ivan, married him to the Princess, and made him his heir. The wedding feast began again and they sent for the ancient old sailormen to take part in it. The ancient old sailormen wept with joy when they saw Ivan and the Princess, like two sweet pigeons sitting side by side. Yes, they lifted their flagons with their old shaking hands and cheered with their old cracked voices and poured the wine down their dry, old throats.

There was wine enough to spare, and beer too, and mead—enough to drown a herd of cattle. As the guests drank and grew merry and proud they set to boasting. This one bragged of his riches, and that one of his wife. Another boasted of his cunning, another of his new house, another of his strength, and this one was angry because they would not let him show how he could lift the table on one hand. They all drank to Ivan's health and he drank to theirs. In the end he could not bear to listen to their proud boasts.

"That's all very well," said he, "but I am the only man in the world who rode on the shoulders of a giant to come to his wedding feast."

The words were scarcely out of his mouth before there was a tremendous trampling and a roar of a great wind. The house shook with the footsteps of the giant as he strode up. The giant bent down over the courtyard and looked in at the feast.

"Little man, little man," said he, "you promised not to boast of me. I told you what would come if you did and here you are and have boasted already."

"Forgive me," said Ivan. "It was the drink that boasted, not I."

"What sort of drink is it that knows how to boast?" said the giant.

"You shall taste it," said Ivan.

He made his ancient old sailormen roll a great barrel of wine into the yard, more than enough for a hundred men. After that, a barrel of beer that was as big and then a barrel of mead that was no smaller.

"Try the taste of that," said Ivan the Ninny.

The giant did not wait to be asked twice. He lifted the barrel of wine as if it had been a little glass and emptied it down his throat. He lifted the barrel of beer as if it had been an acorn and emptied it after the wine. Then he lifted the barrel of mead as if it had been a very small pea and swallowed every drop of mead that was in it. After that he began stamping about and breaking things. Houses fell to pieces this way and that and trees were swept flat like grass. Every step the giant took was followed by the crash of breaking timbers. Suddenly he fell flat on his back and slept. For three days and nights he slept without waking. At last he opened his eyes.

"Just look about you," said Ivan. "See the damage that you've done."

"And did that little drop of drink make me do all that?" said the giant. "Well, well, I can well understand that a drink like that can do a bit of bragging. After that," said he, looking at the wrecks of houses and all the broken things scattered about—"after that," said he, "you can boast of me for a thousand years and I'll have nothing against you."

With that, he tugged at his great whiskers and wrinkled his eyes and went striding off into the sea.

This is the story about salt, and how it made a rich man of Ivan the Ninny, and, besides, gave him the prettiest wife in the world, and she a Tzar's daughter.

The Magic Mill

*(Finland)**

IN THE DAYS WHEN STONES WERE TURNIPS and kept growing and growing, and the sky was so low that it had to be propped up with an old soup spoon, there lived two brothers, one of whom was poor and the other rich. With his neighbors, the rich brother was friendly and ready to please, but with his own brother he acted as if he did not know him, for he feared that the other might come to him a-begging.

Not that the poor brother ever asked anything of the rich one—he never did. That is, unless he could help it.

But once a holiday came along and the younger brother had nothing in the house and his wife said to him, "How are we going to celebrate the holiday? Go to your brother and borrow a little meat from him. He slaughtered a cow yesterday. I know because I saw him doing it."

The poor man did not like to go to his brother and he told his wife so, but there was nowhere else he could go for food. He dragged his feet in the road, kicking up dust as he went to the house of his rich brother. "Lend me a little meat, Brother. We have nothing in the house for the holiday," he asked his older brother.

His rich brother threw him a cow's hoof, crying, "Here, take it and go to Hiisi!"

The younger brother left his rich brother's house and he said to himself, "He has given the hoof not to me, but to Hiisi the Wood Goblin, so to Hiisi I had better take it." And he started off for the forest.

Whether he walked long in the forest or not, no one knows. By and by he met some woodcutters. "Where are you going?" asked the woodcutters.

*From *The Enchanted Wood and Other Tales from Finland* by Norma J. and George Livo. Englewood, Colo.: Libraries Unlimited, 1999.

"To Hiisi the Wood Goblin, to give him this cow's hoof," the poor man answered. "Can you tell me where I can find his hut?"

"Go straight ahead, never swerving from the road, and you'll come to it. But first, listen carefully to us. If Hiisi tries to repay you in silver for the cow's hoof, don't take it. If he tries to give you gold, don't take the gold either. Ask for his millstone and for nothing else."

"Kiitos" (thank you), said the poor man. "Thank you for your kind advice. Goodbye." The poor fellow went on, carefully carrying the cow's hoof.

Whether he walked long or not, nobody knows, but by and by he saw a hut. He knocked on the door, and who answered his knock but Hiisi himself! Hiisi looked at the man and said, "People often promise to bring me gifts, but they rarely do. What is it that you have brought for me?"

"A cow's hoof," was the man's reply as he held out the cow's hoof to Hiisi.

"A cow's hoof?" declared Hiisi. "For thirty years I have eaten no meat," he cried. "Give me the hoof quickly. I am overjoyed." He snatched the hoof and gulped it down.

"Ah, now I should like to pay you for it," Hiisi said. "Do you want much for it? Here, take these two handfuls of silver."

"I don't want any silver," answered the poor man as he remembered the woodcutters' instructions.

Then Hiisi took out some gold chunks and offered the man two handfuls.

"I don't want any gold either," said the poor man.

"What do you want then?" bellowed Hiisi.

"Just your millstone," replied the man.

"Oh no, you can't have that. But I can give you as much money as you like," snarled Hiisi.

The poor man would not agree and kept asking for the millstone just as the woodcutters had told him to do.

"I have eaten the cow's hoof," Hiisi said, "and I suppose I will have to pay you for it. So be it! Take my millstone, but do you know what to do with it?"

"No, I don't," answered the poor man. "Will you tell me what to do?"

"Well," said Hiisi. "This is no simple millstone. It will give you whatever you tell it to give you. You only need to say, 'Grind, my millstone!' If you want it to stop, just say, 'Enough and have done!' and the millstone will stop. Now, be off with you. You have driven a hard deal."

"Kiitos!" said the poor man as he thanked Hiisi. He set off homewards with his millstone. For a long time he walked in the forest. He walked until it grew dark. Then rain fell in torrents. The wind whistled, and the branches of trees struck him in the face and on his shoulders. It was morning by the time the poor man came home.

"Where have you been wandering all day and all night?" asked his wife. "I was beginning to think that I might never see you again."

"You'll never guess where I was! I was at the house of Hiisi the Wood Goblin himself," blurted the poor man. "See what he has given me." With that, he took the millstone out of his bag.

"Grind, my millstone!" he told it. "Give us nice things to eat for the holiday."

The millstone began, of itself, to turn round and round. Flour, grain, sugar, meat, fish, and everything else one could wish for poured onto the table. The poor man's wife brought sacks and bowls and baskets, and she filled them full of food.

The poor man tapped the millstone with his finger and said, "Enough and have done!" and the millstone stopped grinding at once and came to a standstill.

The poor man's family had as good a holiday as anyone in the village. Their life from that time changed for the better. There was enough and to spare in the house, so the wife and children had fine new clothes and shoes. They wanted for nothing.

One day the poor man ordered his millstone to grind him a good measure of oats for his horse. The millstone did so. The horse ate the oats as he stood by the house.

Just then, the rich brother sent his workman to the lake to water his horses. The workman drove the horses to the lake, but as they were passing the poor brother's house they stopped and began eating oats alongside the poor man's horse.

The rich brother saw them from his house and he came out onto his porch. "Hey there!" he called to his workman. "Lead the horses away at once! They are picking up sweepings and they will get sick!"

The workman brought back the horses. "You were wrong, master," he said. "Those were not sweepings, but the choicest oats I have ever seen. Your brother has oats and everything else in abundance."

This aroused the rich brother's curiosity. "I think I will go and see how such a miracle could have possibly come to pass. How has my brother suddenly become rich?" wondered the rich man. He went over to his brother's house to see for himself.

"How have you become rich all of a sudden?" he asked his brother. "Where did all these good things I see come from?"

The poor brother told him honestly, "Hiisi helped me," he said.

"What do you mean?" the rich brother asked.

"Exactly what I said. You gave me a cow's hoof on the eve of the holiday and told me to go to Hiisi with it. That is just what I did. I gave Hiisi the hoof, and in return, he made me a present of a magic millstone. It is this millstone that gives me everything I ask for."

"Show me this magic millstone," demanded his brother.

"As you wish," said the poor brother. He ordered the millstone to give them delicacies of all sorts to eat. The millstone at once began turning and it loaded the table with piirakkaa, smoked salmon, cakes, roasted meats, and lots of other good things.

The rich brother just stood there with his eyes and mouth wide open. "Sell me the millstone," he begged his brother.

"Oh no," answered the poor brother. "I need it myself."

But the rich brother wouldn't take no for an answer. "Name your price, only sell it to me!" he urged.

"I told you it is not for sale," the poor man repeated.

The rich brother realized he would not gain anything by badgering his brother, so he tried a different approach. "Was there ever anyone as ungrateful as you!" he cried. "Who gave you the cow's hoof in the first place?"

"It was you, of course," answered the poor brother.

"There you are then! You begrudge me the millstone," wheedled the rich brother. "Well, if you won't sell it to me, at least lend it to me for a while."

The poor brother thought over this request. "Have it your own way," he finally said. "You can borrow it for a spell."

The rich brother was delighted. He seized the millstone and ran home with it, without ever thinking as to what was required to make it stop turning.

The very next morning he put out to sea in a boat, taking the millstone with him. "Everyone is salting fish right now," he thought to himself. "Salt is expensive so I will trade in salt and get rich." He was well out to sea by now so he told the millstone, "Grind, my millstone! I need salt and the more the better."

The millstone started spinning and turning and the purest, whitest salt poured from it. The rich man looked on in glee, rubbing his hands together as he calculated how rich he would become. It was high time to tell the millstone to stop, but all he did was to repeat from time to time, "Grind, my millstone, grind, don't stop."

The salt began to get so deep and heavy that the boat settled deeper and deeper in the water. The rich brother seemed to have taken leave of his senses, for he did nothing but repeat the words, "Grind, my millstone, grind!"

By now the water was gushing over the sides of the boat and sloshing over the salt. The boat was near to sinking and the older brother suddenly came to his senses. "Stop grinding, millstone," he shouted.

But the millstone went on grinding as before.

"Stop grinding, millstone! Stop grinding right now, I say," the rich man shouted again. The millstone went right on grinding unceasingly. The rich brother tried to snatch up the millstone and throw it overboard, but it seemed to have grown fast to the deck, for he could not lift it. He could not budge it.

"Help!" screamed the rich brother. "Save me! Help!" There was no one there to save him and no one there to help him.

The boat sank, taking the rich brother with it into the watery deep and the sea closed over him, the boat, and the millstone.

Whatever happened to the millstone? They say that even at the bottom of the sea it never stopped grinding and it just makes more and more and more salt. That, believe it or not, is why seawater is salty!

Food for Thought

- Interview a chef. Find out how/why that person became a chef. Share what you discovered with others.
- Visit a grocery store. List all the spices you find there. Check your home spice shelves as well. What spices are there? How many of them do you and your family use at home in cooking? Share the recipes with others.
- Discover where some of these spices are grown. How do the people of that specific region utilize the spices? Are there any holidays or celebrations that revolve around particular spices?
- Check your local newspapers for their weekly food sections (usually Wednesday's issue). Collect recipes and articles that use a variety of spices.
- Prepare a recipe and plan a potluck with your class, friends, or family. Sample all the various dishes and try to guess what spices were added.
- Develop a science project in which you experiment with growing herbs.
- Keep a log detailing the changes in your herbs (color, size, shape, smell, etc.). Note the amounts of sun exposure and the levels of watering that each herb receives. Compare one herb to another. Observe growth speeds, size, shape, smell, and medicinal uses.
- Use the herbs you have grown for tasting and cooking. Create a collection of recipes that require that herb.

- ▲ Ask the librarian to help you find a map of where spices come from. Find recipes of several of your favorite foods. Show on a blank world map where the different spices in these dishes came from.
- ▲ Discover some of the medicinal uses other cultures have made of herbs and spices. Some herbs to investigate are sage, mint, thyme, and rosemary.
- ▲ Columbus promised to open up new spice routes in order to get financial support for his voyage. Why might this have been an important reason for his exploration?
- ▲ Develop a list of questions you have about herbs and spices. Make arrangements to visit a local greenhouse or garden shop and get answers to some of these questions. Create a presentation on your findings.
- ▲ Research some of the uses of salt and where it is found. Is it only useful for food? Do humans and animals need salt to survive? Are there any animals that do not? If so, which ones and why?
- ▲ As a group project, develop a book about herbs and spices that is factual as well as literary. Add your own stories and poems to this book.

Part Six

Magic and Trickery

Hansel and Gretel

(Brothers Grimm)

NEAR A GREAT FOREST there lived a poor woodcutter, his wife, and his two children by his dead first wife. The boy's name was Hansel and the girl's, Gretel. They had little to bite or to sup, and once, when there was a great dearth in the land, the man could not even gain their daily bread.

As he lay in bed one night thinking of this and turning and tossing, he sighed heavily and said to his wife: "What will become of us? We cannot even feed our children. There is nothing left for ourselves."

"I will tell you what, Husband," answered the wife. "We will take the children early in the morning into the forest where it is thickest. We will make them a fire, and we will give each of them a piece of bread. Then we will go to our work and leave them alone. They will never find the way home again, and we shall be quit of them."

"No, Wife," said the man. "I cannot do that. I cannot find it in my heart to take my children into the forest and leave them there alone. The wild animals would soon come and devour them."

"Oh, you fool," said she. "Then we will all four starve. You had better get the coffins ready." She left him no peace until he consented.

"But I really pity the poor children," said the man.

The two children had not been able to sleep for hunger and had heard what their stepmother had said to their father. Gretel wept bitterly and said to Hansel, "It is all over with us."

"Do be quiet, Gretel," said Hansel, "and do not fret. I will manage something."

When the parents had gone to sleep, he got up, put on his little coat, opened the back door, and slipped out. The moon was shining brightly, and the white flints that lay in front of the house glistened like pieces of silver. Hansel stooped and filled the little pockets of his coat as full as he could. Then he went back inside again and said to Gretel: "Be easy, dear little Sister, and go to sleep quietly. God will not forsake us." And he laid himself down again in his bed.

When the day was breaking and before the sun had risen, the wife came and awakened the two children, saying: "Get up, you lazy bones. We are going into the forest to cut wood."

Then she gave each of them a piece of bread and said, "That is for dinner, and you must not eat it before then, for you will get no more."

Gretel carried the bread under her apron, for Hansel had his pockets full of the flints. Then they set off all together on their way to the forest. When they had gone a little way, Hansel stood still and looked back toward the house, and this he did again and again, till his father said to him: "Hansel, what are you looking at? Take care not to forget your legs."

"Oh, Father," said Hansel, "I am looking at my little white kitten, who is sitting up on the roof to bid me good-bye."

"You young fool," said the woman. "That is not your kitten but the sunshine on the chimney pot."

Of course, Hansel had not been looking at his kitten but had been taking every now and then a flint, a hard dark stone, from his pocket and dropping it on the road.

When they reached the middle of the forest, the father told the children to collect wood to make a fire to keep them warm, and Hansel and Gretel gathered brushwood enough for a little mountain. They set it on fire, and when the flame was burning quite high the wife said, "Now lie down by the fire and rest yourselves, you children, and we will go and cut wood. When we are ready, we will come and fetch you."

So Hansel and Gretel sat by the fire, and at noon they each ate their pieces of bread. They thought their father was in the wood all the time, as they seemed to hear the stroke of an ax, but really it was only a dry branch hanging from a withered tree that the wind moved to and fro. So when they had stayed there a long time, their eyelids closed with weariness, and they fell fast asleep.

When at last they woke, it was night. Gretel began to cry, and she said, "How shall we ever get out of this wood?"

Hansel comforted her, saying, "Wait a little while longer, until the moon rises, and then we can easily find the way home."

And when the full moon came up, Hansel took his little sister by the hand and followed the way where the flint stones shone like silver and showed them the road. They walked on the whole night through, and at the break of day they came to their father's house. They knocked at the door, and when the wife opened it and saw it was Hansel and Gretel, she said: "You naughty children, why did you sleep so long in the wood? We thought you were never coming home again!" But the father was glad, for it had gone to his heart to leave them both in the woods alone.

Not very long after that there was again great scarcity in those parts, and the children heard their stepmother say at night in bed to their father: "Everything is finished up. We have only half a loaf, and after that the tale comes to an end. The children must be off. We will take them farther into the wood this time so that they shall not be able to find the way back again. There is no other way to manage."

The man felt sad at heart, and he thought it would be better to share one's last morsel with one's children. But the wife would listen to nothing that he said. She scolded and reproached him. When a man has given in once, he has to do it a second time.

But the children were not asleep and had heard all the talk. So when the parents had gone to sleep, Hansel got up to go out and get some more flint stones as he had done before. But the wife had locked the door, and Hansel could not get out. He comforted his little sister and said: "Do not cry, Gretel. Go to sleep quietly, and God will help us."

Early the next morning the wife came and pulled the children out of bed. She gave them each a little piece of bread—less than before. On the way to the wood Hansel crumbled the bread in his pocket and often stopped to throw a crumb on the ground.

"Hansel, what are you stopping behind and staring for?" asked his father.

"I am looking at my little pigeon sitting on the roof and saying good-bye to me," answered Hansel.

"You fool," said the wife. "That is no pigeon but is the morning sun shining on the chimney pots."

Hansel went on as before and strewed bread crumbs all along the road.

The woman led the children far into the wood—farther than they had ever been before. And again they made a large fire, and the stepmother said: "Sit still there, you children. And when you are tired, you can go to sleep. We are going into the forest to cut wood, and in the evening when we are ready to go home, we will come and fetch you."

So when noon came, Gretel shared her bread with Hansel, who had strewed his along the road. Then they went to sleep, and the evening passed, and no one came for the poor children. When they awoke, it was dark night. Hansel comforted his little sister and said: "Wait a little, Gretel, until the moon gets up. Then we shall be able to see the way home by the crumbs of bread that I have scattered on the trail."

So when the moon rose, they got up, but they could find no crumbs of bread, for the birds of the woods and of the fields had come and picked them up. Hansel thought they might find the way all the same, but they could not. They went on all that night and the next day—from the morning until the evening—but they could not find the way out of the woods. They were very hungry, for they had nothing to eat but the few berries they could pick up. And when they were so tired that they could no longer drag themselves along, they lay down under a tree and fell asleep.

It was then the third morning since they had left their father's house. They tried to find their way back, but instead they only found themselves farther in the wood, and if help had not soon come, they would have starved. About noon they saw a pretty snow-white bird sitting on a bough and singing so sweetly that they stopped to listen. And when he had finished the bird spread his wings and flew before them, and they followed after him until they came to a little house. The bird perched on the roof, and when they came nearer, they saw that the house was built of bread and roofed with cakes. The window was of transparent sugar.

"We will have some of this," said Hansel, "and make a fine meal. I will eat a piece of the roof, Gretel, and you can have some of the window—that will taste sweet."

So Hansel reached up and broke off a bit of the roof just to see how it tasted, and Gretel stood by the window and gnawed at it. Then they heard a thin voice call out from inside,

Nibble, nibble, like a mouse
Who is nibbling at my house?

And the children answered,

Never mind,
It is the wind.

And they went on eating, never disturbing themselves. Hansel, who found that the roof tasted very nice, took down a great piece of it, and Gretel pulled out a large round windowpane. They sat themselves down and began to eat. Then the door opened and an aged woman came out, leaning on a crutch. Hansel and Gretel felt frightened and let fall what they had in their hands. The old woman, however, nodded her head and asked: "Ah, my dear children, how come you here? You must come indoors and stay with me. You will be no trouble."

So she took each by the hand and led them into her little house. There they found a good meal laid out of milk and pancakes with sugar, apples, and nuts. After they had eaten, the old woman showed them two little white beds, and Hansel and Gretel laid themselves down on them and thought they were in heaven.

The old woman, although her behavior was so kind, was a wicked witch, who lay in wait for children and had built the little house to entice them. When they were once inside, she used to kill them, cook them, and eat them, and then it was a feast day with her. The witch's eyes were red, and she could not see very far, but she had a keen scent, like the beasts, and knew very well when human creatures were near. When she had seen that Hansel and Gretel were coming, she had given a spiteful laugh and had said triumphantly, "I have them, and they shall not escape me!"

Early in the morning, before the children were awake, she got up to look at them. As they lay sleeping so peacefully with round rosy cheeks, she said to herself, What a fine feast I shall have!

Then she grasped Hansel with her withered hand and led him into a little stable and shut him up behind a grating. Call and scream as he might, it did no good. Then she went back to Gretel and shook her, crying, "Get up, lazy bones, fetch water and cook something nice for your brother. He is outside in the stable and must be fattened up. And when he is fat enough I will eat him."

Gretel began to weep bitterly, but it was no use. She had to do what the wicked witch bade her.

And so the best kinds of victuals were cooked for poor Hansel, while Gretel got nothing but crab shells. Each morning the old woman visited the little stable and cried, "Hansel, stretch out your finger so that I may tell if you will soon be fat enough to eat."

Hansel, however, used to hold out a little bone, and the old woman, who had weak eyes, could not see what it was. Supposing it to be Hansel's finger, she wondered that it was not getting fatter. When four weeks had passed and Hansel seemed to remain so thin, she lost patience and could wait no longer.

"Now then, Gretel," cried she to the little girl. "Be quick and draw water. Be Hansel fat or be he lean, tomorrow I must kill and cook him."

Oh, what a grief for the poor little sister to have to fetch water, and how the tears flowed down over her cheeks! "Dear God, pray help us!" cried she. "If we had been devoured by wild beasts in the wood, at least we should have died together."

"Spare me your lamentations," said the old woman. "They are of no avail."

Early the next morning Gretel had to get up, make the fire, and fill the kettle. "First we will do the baking," said the old woman. "I have heated the oven already and kneaded the dough."

She pushed poor Gretel toward the oven, out of which the flames were already shining. "Creep in," said the witch, "and see if it is properly hot so that the bread may be baked."

With Gretel in the oven the witch meant to shut the door upon her and let her be baked, and then she would have eaten her. But Gretel perceived her intention and said: "I don't know how to do it. How shall I get in?"

"Stupid goose," said the old woman. "The opening is big enough, do you see? I could get in myself." And then she stooped down and put her head in the oven's mouth. Then Gretel gave her a push so that she went in farther, and she shut the iron door upon her and put up the bar. Oh, how frightfully the witch howled! But Gretel ran away and left the wicked witch to burn miserably. Gretel went straight to Hansel, opened the stable door, and cried: "Hansel, we are free! The old witch is dead!"

Then out flew Hansel like a bird from its cage as soon as the door was opened. How happy they both were! How they fell each on the other's neck and danced about and kissed each other! And as they had nothing more to fear, they went all over the old witch's house and found that in every corner there stood chests of pearls and precious stones.

"This is something better than flint stones," said Hansel as he filled his pockets. Gretel, thinking she also would like to carry something home with her, filled her apron full.

"Now, away we go," said Hansel. "If we only can get out of the witch's wood."

When they had journeyed a few hours, they came to a great piece of water. "We can never get across this," said Hansel. "I see no stepping-stones and no bridge."

"And there is no boat either," said Gretel. "But here comes a white duck. If I ask her, she will help us over." So Gretel cried,

Duck, duck, here we stand,
Hansel and Gretel, on the land,
Stepping-stones and bridge we lack,
Carry us over on your nice white back.

And the duck came accordingly, and Hansel got upon her and told his sister to come too. "No," answered Gretel, "that would be too hard upon the duck. We can go separately, one after the other."

And that was how it was managed, and after that they went on happily until they came to the wood. The way grew more and more familiar, till at last they saw in the distance their father's house. Then they ran till they came up to it, rushed in at the door, and fell on their father's neck. The man had not had a quiet hour since he had left his children in the wood. His wife was dead. When Gretel opened her apron, the pearls and precious stones were scattered all over the room, and Hansel took one handful after another out of his pocket. Then was all care at an end, and they lived in great joy together.

Sing every one
My story is done,
And look! round the house
There runs a little mouse.
He that can catch her before she scampers in
May make himself a fur cap out of her skin.

The Magic Pot
(Denmark)

SOMEWHERE BEYOND THE BLUE FOREST, beyond the straw town where they sift water and pour sand, lived a man and his wife. They lived in the smallest and poorest hut in the whole village. The sorry fact was that they were so poor they often went without even their daily bread.

They had sold nearly everything they owned, but managed somehow to keep their only cow. When all else was gone, they knew that the cow must go too. The man led her away to market. As he was walking along the road a stranger came up to him and asked, "Do you plan to sell this animal? If so, how much money do you want for her?"

The man wasn't expecting this question from a stranger, but he gave it just a little bit of thought before he said, "I think, that a hundred crowns would be a fair price."

The stranger answered, "Money I cannot give you. I have something that is worth as much as a hundred crowns, though. Here is a pot that I am willing to trade you for your cow." With a flourish, he showed the man an iron pot with three legs and a handle.

"Indeed! An ordinary pot!" exclaimed the cow's owner. "What possible use would that pot be to me when I have absolutely nothing to put in it? My wife and children cannot eat an iron pot." He sighed, "No, money is what I need and what I must have."

The two men looked at each other and at the cow and at the pot. Then an amazing thing happened. The three-legged pot suddenly began to speak. "Just take me," it said.

The poor man thought that if the pot could speak, surely it could do more than that, so he declared, "Done!" With that, he took the pot and gave the stranger the rope he was using to lead the cow. He took the pot and returned home with it.

The trip back home gave him time to worry about what his wife would say. When he reached his hut, he went to the stall where the cow had been tied. He tied the pot to the manger. Then he went into the hut and asked his wife, "Give me something to eat." It had been a long walk and he was hungry.

"Well, dear husband," said his wife. "Were you able to make a good bargain for the cow at the market? What price did you get?"

"The price was fair enough," replied the man. "I suspect that I made a good deal of it."

"I am so glad to hear that," she said in relief. "The money will help us for a long time until things get better again."

"Well, no," he sighed. "I didn't take money for the cow."

She cried, "Dear me! What did you take for the cow then?"

"Go out to the cow's stall and look. It is tied up to the manger," he instructed her.

The wife went out to the cow's stall and all she could see tied up to the manger was a three-legged black pot. "Where is it, husband?" she asked. When she learned that the pot was what her husband had received in trade for the cow she scolded him. She called him names. She screamed at him, "You are a great blockhead! I wish now that I had taken the cow to market! I never dreamed that you would be this foolish! Now what are we to do?" She went on and on like this for quite a while.

"Clean me and put me on the fire," shouted the pot. "Enough of this!"

The wife blinked her eyes in wonder and now it was her turn to think that if the pot could talk maybe it could do more than that. She carefully took the pot into the kitchen and washed and cleaned it. Then she put the pot on the fire.

"I skip, I skip!" cried the pot.

"How far do you skip?" asked the woman.

"To the rich man's house, to the rich man's house," it answered as it ran from the fireplace to the door, across the yard, and up the road as fast as its three short legs could carry it. The rich man, who had never shared anything with the poor, lived not too far away. The rich man's wife was baking bread when the pot came running in and jumped up on the table.

"Ah," spoke the woman. "Isn't this wonderful! I need you for a pudding which must be baked at once." Thereupon she began to heap good things into the pot. She put in flour, sugar, butter, raisins, almonds, spices, and other good things. The pot sat quietly as she put everything in it. When the ingredients for the pudding were finished, the rich man's wife reached for the pot, intending to put it on the stove.

Tap, tap, tap, went the three short legs of the pot and the pot stood on the threshold of the open door. "Mercy me, oh my! Where are you going with my pudding?" called the woman.

The pot replied, "To the poor man's house," and it ran down the road just as fast as its three little legs could go. When the poor couple saw the pot skipping back to them with everything for a pudding in it, they rejoiced. "Now," asked the husband, "was the bargain I made for the cow not a good one?"

His wife was pleased and contented and could only agree, "Yes." The next morning the pot cried again, "I skip, I skip!"

"How far do you skip this time?" they asked.

"To the rich man's barn!" it shouted. They watched it run up the road. When it arrived at the rich man's barn it hopped through the doorway.

There were some men threshing wheat. "Look at that black pot!" they cried. "Let's see how much it will hold." They poured a bushel of wheat into it, but it didn't seem to be full so they got another bushel and added that to it, but there was still more room. When every grain of wheat had been put in the pot, it still looked as if it could hold more. It still wasn't full. Once there was no more wheat to be found, the three short legs of the pot began to move. When the men looked around, the pot had already reached the gate.

"Where are you going with our wheat? Stop, stop!" they called out to the pot.

"I am going to the poor man's home," answered the pot. It skipped and sped down the road, leaving the men behind, dumbfounded and dismayed.

Again, the poor couple was delighted. The wheat that was in the pot was enough to feed them for several years. On the third morning the pot once more skipped up the road. It was a beautiful day, with the sun shining so brightly that the rich man had taken out his money from where he kept it. He spread it out on a table near an open window to allow the sunshine to kill the mold that was forming on his gold. All at once, the pot stood on the table before him. Like greedy, wealthy men do, he was counting his coins. Even though he had no idea where this three-legged pot came from, he decided that it would make a fine place to store his money. He threw in handfuls of money, one after another, until the pot was holding all of it. At that very moment, the pot jumped from the table to the windowsill.

"Whoa! Stop!" shouted the rich man. "Where are you going with all of my gold?"

"I go to the poor man's home," answered the pot as it skipped down the road. The money inside it was dancing and clinking merrily. The pot stopped in the middle of the poor man's hut and stood there. When the couple saw the fortune that was in it, they cried out in ecstasy.

"Clean me and wash me," said the pot. "Put me aside."

The very next morning the pot announced again that it was ready to skip. "How far do you skip?" asked the couple.

Again, the pot replied, "to the rich man's house." It ran up the road again. It never stopped until it had reached the rich man's kitchen. The rich man was in the kitchen at the time and as soon as he saw the pot he cried, "There is the pot that carried away our pudding, our wheat, and all of our money. I'll make it return everything that it stole!"

The angry man flung himself upon the pot and there he stuck. He wasn't able to pull himself off. "I skip, I skip!" shouted the pot.

"Skip to the North Pole if you want," shouted the rich man. He was furiously trying to free himself, but the three short legs of the pot kept dancing along, carrying the rich man, flailing away, down the road.

The poor man and his wife saw the pot pass their door and could see that it wasn't going to stop. For all that anyone knows, the pot went straight on, carrying the rich man to the North Pole.

It didn't matter because the poor couple was now rich. They often thought about the wonderful pot with the three short legs, which had skipped so joyfully for their good. It was gone, though, and they have never seen it since. I am glad that we have come to the end of the story and we can all have a rest.

Sweet Porridge

(Brothers Grimm)

There was a poor but good little girl who lived alone with her mother, and they no longer had anything to eat. So the child went into the forest, and there an aged woman met her who was aware of her sorrow. The woman presented her with a little pot which, when she said, "Cook, little pot, cook," would cook good, sweet porridge, and when she said, "Stop, little pot," ceased to cook. The girl took the pot home to her mother, and now they were freed from their poverty and hunger and ate sweet porridge as often as they chose.

Once when the girl had gone out, her mother said, "Cook, little pot, cook." And it did cook and she ate till she was satisfied, and then she wanted the pot to stop cooking, but did not know the word. So it went on cooking and the porridge rose over the edge, and still it cooked on until the kitchen and whole house were full, and then the next house, and then the whole street, just as if it wanted to satisfy the hunger of the whole world, and there was the greatest distress, but no one knew how to stop it.

At last when only one single house remained, the child came home and just said, "Stop, little pot," and it stopped and gave up cooking, and whosoever wished to return to the town had to eat his way back.

The Orphan Boy and the Monkeys
(Hmong of Southeast Asia)

Thousands of years ago, there was an orphan who lived with his elder brother and sister-in-law. His sister-in-law didn't like him and resented his living with them. In fact, she planned to kill him. The orphan cried and was very sad because he knew he was not wanted, and besides that, he was lonely.

One of the nasty things his sister-in-law did was to give him dried seeds to plant. Everyone knows that dried seeds are no good for growing things. However, he didn't have any other seeds to plant, so he sowed all of them in the field. Of course, many of them did not grow, but surprisingly, some of the seeds did sprout.

As the plants in his garden grew and the grain ripened, the monkeys kept stealing his corn and rice. The orphan decided to ask the shoa, or wise man, for his help.

"Why do the monkeys keep coming to take all of my corn?" the orphan asked the shoa. "I work hard taking care of a very poor crop and I can't make the monkeys stay away. I am poor! I need all the crops I can grow. What am I to do?"

"Go home, kill a chicken, cook it, and eat some of it. Put some of what is left in your nose, your eyes, and your ears. You know how quickly things rot in our jungle. As the chicken pieces rot, they will start to smell. In fact the chicken in your stomach will start to make gas and add to the smell," counseled the wise man. "Then go to the path made by the monkeys and lay down on the path. Go to sleep right there in the middle of it."

The orphan did as the wise man had told him. He killed a chicken, boiled it in water, and ate some of it. Afterwards he put some of the chicken pieces on his eyes, in his ears, and in his nose. He found the monkey's trail and laid down in the middle of it and had no trouble falling asleep.

The monkeys found him on the trail and thought he was dead. "Who died here? He surely does smell," they said. They picked the orphan up and carried him to the mountains where they lived. The monkeys had a big funeral ceremony for the dead farmer and invited many animals to come and join them. All the animals that came brought gold and money to put around the orphan as he lay on the blanket. They beat the drum and played the keng, or reed instrument.

Suddenly, the farmer sat up and lunged at the animals, yelling, "Yah-h-h-h!" as loudly as he could. All of the shocked and frightened animals ran away. The monkeys clambered up into the trees.

Then the orphan calmly picked up all of the gold and silver and went home a rich man. When he got to the home of his brother and sister-in-law and showed them the fortune, they asked him, "Where did you get all of these riches?"

The orphan told them the story of the monkeys and how he had gone to the shoa for advice. He explained how he had tricked the monkeys. And so the orphan lived with his family and shared his wealth with them. He was never sad or lonely again and his sister-in-law made sure she treated him very nice so he wouldn't think of leaving them. That was how the orphan found happiness thousands of years ago.

The Turnip
*(Brothers Grimm)**

There were once two brothers who served as soldiers. One was rich and the other poor. The poor one, to escape from his poverty, put off his soldier's coat and turned farmer. He dug and hoed his bit of land and sowed it with turnip seed. The seed came up, and one turnip grew there that became large and vigorous and grew visibly bigger and bigger. It seemed as if it would never stop growing. It might have been called the princess of turnips, for never was such a turnip seen before, and never will such a turnip be seen again.

It finally became so enormous that it filled a whole cart, and two oxen were required to draw it. The farmer had not the least idea what he was to do with the turnip or whether it would be a fortune to him or a misfortune. At last he thought: If I sell it, what will I get for it? I could eat it myself, but the small turnips would taste just as good. It would be better to take it to the king and make him a present of it.

So he placed it on a cart, harnessed two oxen, took it to the palace, and presented it to the king. "What strange thing is this?" asked the king. "Many wonderful things have come before my eyes, but never such a monster as this! From what seed can this have sprung, or are you a luck child and have met with it by chance?"

"Ah, no!" said the farmer. "No luck child am I. I am a poor soldier, who, because he could no longer support himself, hung his soldier's coat on a nail and took to farming land. I have a brother who is rich and well-known to you, lord king. But I, because I have nothing, am forgotten by

*From *Who's Afraid ... Facing Children's Fears Through Folktales* by Norma J. Livo. Englewood, Colo.: Libraries Unlimited, 1994.

everyone." Then the king felt compassion for him, and said, "You shall be raised from poverty and shall have such gifts from me that you shall be equal to your rich brother." The king bestowed on him much gold, lands, meadows, and herds and made him immensely rich. The wealth of the other brother could not be compared with his.

When the rich brother heard what the poor one had gained for himself with one single turnip, he envied him and thought in every way how he also could get hold of a similar piece of luck. He would, however, set about it in a much wiser way. He took gold and horses and carried them to the king. He wanted to make certain the king would give him a much larger present in return. If his brother had got so much for one turnip, what would he not carry away with him in return for such beautiful things as these? The king accepted his present and said that he had nothing to give him in return that was more rare and excellent than the great turnip.

So the rich man was obliged to put his brother's turnip in a cart and have it taken to his home. When there, he did not know on whom to vent his rage and anger. But then bad thoughts came to him, and he resolved to kill his brother. He hired murderers, who were to ambush his brother, and then he went to his brother and said: "Dear brother, I know of a hidden treasure. We will dig it up together and divide it between us." The other agreed to this and accompanied him without suspicion. While they were on their way, however, the murderers fell on him, bound him, and would have hung him from a tree. But just as they were about to do this, loud singing and the sound of a horse's feet were heard in the distance. On this their hearts were filled with terror, and they pushed their prisoner head-first into a sack, hung it on a branch, and took flight. He, however, worked up there until he had made a hole in the sack through which he could put his head.

The man who was coming by was no other than a traveling student, a young fellow who, on his way through the wood, joyously sang his song. When he who was aloft saw that someone was passing below him, he cried: "Good day! You have come at a lucky time."

The student looked around on every side but did not know where the voice was coming from. At last he called, "Who speaks?"

An answer came from the top of the tree: "Raise your eyes. Here I sit in the Sack of Knowledge. In a short time I have learned great things. Compared with this, all schools are a jest. In a very short time I shall have learned everything and shall descend wiser than all other men. I understand the stars and the signs of the zodiac and the tracks of the winds and the sand of the sea and the healing of illness and the virtues of all herbs, birds, and stones. If you were once within it, you would feel what noble things issue forth from the Sack of Knowledge."

When he heard all this the student was astonished and said: "Blessed be the hour in which I have found you! May not I also enter the sack for a while?"

An unwilling reply came from above: "For a short time I will let you get into it if you reward me and give me good words. You must wait an hour longer, for one thing remains that I must learn before I do it."

The student waited. He became impatient and begged to be allowed to get in at once. His thirst for knowledge was consuming him.

He who was above pretended at last to yield and said, "In order that I may come forth from the house of knowledge you must let it down by the rope, and then you shall enter it."

So the student let the sack down, untied it, and set him free, and then he cried, "Now, draw me up at once!" He was about to get into the sack.

"Halt!" cried the other. "That will not do." And he took him by the head and put him upside down into the sack, fastened it, and drew the disciple of wisdom up the tree by the rope. He swung the student in the air and asked: "How goes it with you, my dear fellow? Behold, already you feel wisdom coming and are gaining valuable experience. Keep perfectly quiet until you become wiser." With this he mounted the student's horse and rode away, but in an hour's time sent someone to let the student out again.

Donkey Cabbages
(Germany)

A HAPPY YOUNG HUNTSMAN went into the forest to hunt. As he went through the woods he whistled and hummed in joyful anticipation of a good hunt. Suddenly, before him appeared an ugly old crone who came up to him. "Good day, dear huntsman. You are merry and contented according to your joyous whistling and humming. But, as for me, I am suffering from hunger and thirst. I beg of you to give me some charity."

The young huntsman felt sorry for the old woman, so he reached into his pocket and felt for some money. He gave her what he could afford and was about to leave.

The old woman stopped him and said, "Listen, dear huntsman, to what I tell you. I will give you a present in return for your kindness. Go on your way now, but in a little while you will come to a tree that has nine birds sitting on it. They will have a cloak in their claws and will be plucking at it. Take your gun and shoot into the midst of them. They will let the cloak fall down to you but one of the birds will be hurt. It will drop down dead. Take the cloak, for it is a wishing-cloak. You will only have to throw it over your shoulders and make a wish to be in a certain place and you will be there in the twinkling of an eye. Take out the heart of the dead bird and swallow it whole. Every morning when you get up, you will find a gold piece under your pillow."

The huntsman thanked the wise woman and thought to himself, "Those are fine things that she has promised me if all she said comes true." With that he walked about a hundred paces, when he heard in the tree branches above him a screaming and twittering. He looked up and saw there a crowd of birds tearing a piece of cloth with their beaks and claws. They were tugging and fighting as if each wanted to have it all to himself.

"Well," said the huntsman, "this is wonderful. It has really come to pass just as the old woman told me!" He took the gun from his shoulder, aimed, and fired right into the middle of the birds. Feathers flew all about. The birds instantly took to flight with loud outcries but, just as the woman had said, one dropped down dead. The cloak fell down at the same time. The huntsman did just as the woman had told him. He cut open the bird, found the heart, swallowed it down, and took the cloak home with him.

The next morning he was eager to see if the old woman's promise had been fulfilled. He lifted up the pillow, and there was a gold piece shining in his eyes. The next day he found another, and so it went each morning when he got up. He gathered together a heap of gold, but at last he thought, "What use is all my gold to me if I stay at home? I will go out and travel the world."

He said goodbye to his family, buckled on his huntsman's pouch and gun, and went off to see the world. One day as he traveled through a dense forest and was almost at the end of it, there was a plain before him. And right there in the plain stood a fine castle.

He could see an old woman standing at one of the windows, with a beautiful maiden. The old woman was a witch. "Ah ha! A man is coming out of the forest and he has a wonderful treasure in his body. We must steal it from him, my dear daughter. It is much more suitable for us than for him. He has a bird's heart within him, and because of it, each morning a gold piece lies under his pillow."

The witch told her daughter what she was to do to get it. She also threatened her daughter, "And if you don't attend to what I say, it will be all the worse for you."

When the huntsman came nearer, he saw how really beautiful the young girl was. "I have traveled about for such a long time. I will take a rest now and enter that beautiful castle. I certainly have enough money," he thought. Of course, the real reason was that he wanted to see more of the enchanting young girl.

He entered the castle and was graciously and courteously welcomed. Before long he was so much in love with the young witch that he no longer thought of anything else. He saw things as the girl saw them and did everything she desired.

The old woman said, "It is time now. We must have the bird's heart. He will never miss it." The old witch prepared a drink and when it was ready, she poured it into a cup. She gave the cup to the maiden, who was to present it to the huntsman.

"My dearest, here is a special drink for you. I want you to drink to me," said the girl. The huntsman took the cup and after he had swallowed the drink, he threw up the heart of the bird. The girl managed to take it away secretly and swallow it herself, because that was what the old woman had told her to do.

The next morning there was no gold beneath the pillow of the huntsman. It was the same each day. However, under the pillow of the maiden, each morning she found a gold coin. The old woman took it away from the young girl each morning.

Even with the absence of the gold, the young huntsman was so lovestruck he thought of nothing else but of passing his time with the girl.

The old witch said, "We have the bird's heart, but we must also take the wishing-cloak away from him."

The girl answered her, "Let us leave him that. He has lost his wealth."

"Such a cloak is a wonderful thing. It is seldom to be found in this world. I must and I will have it!" angrily spoke the witch. She struck the girl several times and said that if she did not obey, things would fare ill for her.

The maiden did the old woman's bidding. She placed herself at the window and gazed on the distant country as if she were very sorrowful. The huntsman saw her and asked, "Why are you standing there so sorrowfully?"

"Ah, my beloved," she answered, "over yonder lies the Garnet Mountain, where the precious stones grow. I long for them so much that when I think of them I feel quite sad. Who could get them for me? Only the birds. They fly and can reach them but a man could never manage to get them."

"Well now, have you nothing else to complain of?" asked the huntsman. "If that is all I will soon remove that burden from your heart."

He drew the maiden under his cloak, wished himself on the Garnet Mountain, and in the twinkling of an eye they were sitting on it together. Precious stones were glistening on every side so that it was a joy to see them. They gathered the finest and richest of them.

The old witch, through her sorceries, caused the eyes of the huntsman to become heavy and close. Suddenly feeling weary, he said to the maiden, "We will sit down and rest awhile. I am so tired that I can no longer stand on my feet." They sat down and he laid his head in her lap and fell asleep.

When he was sound asleep, she unfastened the cloak from his shoulders and wrapped herself in it. She picked up the garnets and other jewels and wished herself back at home with them.

When the huntsman awoke, he saw that his sweetheart had tricked him and left him alone on the wild mountain. "Oh, what treachery there is in the world," he moaned. He sat down there in sorrow. He didn't know what to do. Some wild and monstrous giants lived on the mountain, and he hadn't sat there holding his head in sorrow very long when he saw three of them coming toward him. He lay down and pretended he was in a deep sleep.

When the giants came up, the first kicked him with his foot and said, "What sort of an earthworm is lying curled up here?"

The second giant said, "Step upon him and kill him."

The third giant said, "That would indeed be worth your while. Just let him live. He cannot stay here. When he climbs higher towards the summit of the mountain, the clouds will clutch him and take him away."

After saying all that, they passed the huntsman by. But the huntsman had heard what they said and decided, as soon as they were gone, to climb up to the summit. When he got there, he sat for a while. A cloud floated towards him, caught him up, carried him away, and traveled about for a long time in the heavens. Then it sank lower and let itself down on a great cabbage garden. There were walls all around it. The cloud had let him down to the ground softly on cabbages and vegetables.

The huntsman looked around him and said, "If I only had something to eat! I am so hungry. I don't see apples or pears or any other sort of fruit here. Everywhere there is nothing but cabbages." After a while he thought, "In a pinch I can eat some of the leaves. They will not taste particularly good, but they will at least be food." He picked himself out a fine head of cabbage and ate it. Scarcely had he swallowed a couple of mouthfuls than he felt very strange and quite different.

Four legs grew on him. He also grew a large head and two thick ears. He saw with horror that he had been changed into a donkey. He was still as hungry as ever and since the cabbages were suitable to him in his present condition, he went on eating with great zest. At last he came to a different kind of cabbage. As soon as he swallowed it, he again felt himself change and there he was—in his former human shape.

The huntsman was again very tired, so he lay down and slept. When he awoke the next morning, he broke off one head of the bad cabbages and another of the good ones. "This will help me to get my own again and to punish treachery," he thought. He gathered the cabbages up and climbed over the wall. He started off to find the castle of his sweetheart.

After a couple of days he was lucky enough to find it again. He dyed his face so his own mother wouldn't have known him. He went up to the witch and begged her for shelter. "I am so tired," he said, "that I can go no farther."

"Who are you and what is your business?" asked the witch.

"I am a king's messenger. I was sent out to find the most delicious salad that grows beneath the sun. I have even been so fortunate as to find it and am carrying it with me. The heat of the sun is so intense that the delicate cabbage threatens to whither. I don't know if I can carry it any farther before it spoils." he told her.

When the witch heard of the exquisite salad, she became greedy and said, "Dear fellow, let me just taste this wonderful salad."

"Why not?" answered he. "I have brought two heads with me. I will give you one of them," and he opened his pouch and handed her the bad cabbage.

The witch did not suspect anything and her mouth was watering for this new dish. She herself went into the kitchen to fix it. When it was prepared, she could not wait until it was set on the table but took a couple of leaves at once. She put them in her mouth. Hardly had she swallowed them than she was transformed into a donkey. She ran out into the courtyard.

A maidservant entered the kitchen, saw the salad standing there, and was about to carry it up to the table but on the way, through force of habit, she ate a couple of leaves to taste it. Instantly the magic turned her into a donkey. She too ran out to the courtyard and the old woman. The dish of salad fell to the ground.

The huntsman had gone in and sat down beside the young maiden. Since no one came to the table with the salad, she said, "I don't know what has become of the salad."

The huntsman thought the salad must have already taken effect. He said, "I will go to the kitchen and see what has happened to it." On his way to the kitchen, he looked out a window and saw two donkeys running around in the courtyard. He found the salad lying on the floor. He picked it up, laid it on the dish, and carried them in to the maiden. "I bring you the delicate salad myself," he said, "in order that you won't have to wait any longer."

She ate some of the salad and was immediately transformed into a donkey. She too ran out into the courtyard.

The huntsman washed his face so the donkeys would be able to recognize him. He went down into the courtyard and said to the donkeys, "Now you shall receive the wages of your treachery." He bound them together with a rope and drove them along until he came to a mill. He knocked on the window of the miller's house.

The miller stuck his head out of the window and asked the huntsman what he wanted. "I have three unmanageable beasts," said the huntsman. "I don't want to keep them any longer. Will you take them in and feed them and stable them and manage them as I tell you? I will pay you what you ask."

The miller said, "Why not? How am I to manage them?"

"Give three beatings and one meal daily to the old donkey. Give one beating and three meals to the younger one, and to the youngest, no beatings and three meals," he told the miller. He could not bring himself to have the maiden beaten.

After the deal was done, the huntsman went back to the castle and settled in. After a couple of days, the miller came and told him, "The old donkey is dead. The other two are so sad that they cannot last much longer."

This moved the huntsman to pity and calmed his anger. "Drive them back to me," he told the miller.

When they came home he gave them some of the good cabbage so they became human again. The beautiful girl fell on her knees and said, "My beloved! Forgive me for the evil I have done to you. My mother drove me to it. I did it against my will. I do love you dearly. Your wishing-cloak is in the cupboard and I will vomit up the bird's heart."

The huntsman said, "Keep it. It is all the same, for we will be married and share it all." A great wedding was celebrated and they lived happily together until their death.

The Peachling

(Japan)

IN ANCIENT TIMES there lived in a remote part of Japan a man and his wife. The old man was an honest woodcutter. One day, as was usual, the old man went off to the hills to gather a bundle of sticks while his wife went down to the river to wash the dirty clothes.

The old woman came to the river and put down her dirty clothes. She saw a peach floating down the stream. She waded out into the water to get it, picked it up, and carried it home with her. "What a fine treat this will be for my husband when he comes home," she thought.

After the old man had gathered a bundle of sticks he came down from the hills and back home. His wife set the peach before him with a flourish. Just as she invited him to eat it, the peach split in two and a little howling baby was born into the world.

The old couple took the baby and brought it up as their own. Since it had been born from a peach, they called it Momotaro, or Little Peachling.

Little Peachling grew up to be strong and brave. The three of them lived quite happily except for the fact that there wasn't always enough for them to eat. One day Little Peachling told his parents, "I am going to the Oni's island to carry off the riches that they have stored up there. If you please, I would like some millet dumplings to take along for my journey."

Sadly, the old folks ground the millet and made the dumplings for him. "Goodbye, dear ones," said Little Peachling as they hugged each other goodbye. He cheerfully set out on his travels.

Little Peachling met a monkey along the way. The monkey gibbered at him and said, "Kia! kia! kia! Where are you going, Little Peachling?"

"I am off to the island of the Oni. I plan to find their treasure and carry it away," answered Little Peachling.

"What is that which I see you carrying?" asked the monkey.

"I am carrying the very best millet dumplings in all of Japan. My old parents made them for me specially for this trip," answered Little Peachling.

"Just as I thought!" said the monkey. "If you give me one of them, I will go along with you."

Little Peachling took out one of his dumplings and gave it to the monkey. The monkey eagerly took it and said, "Lead, Little Peachling, and I will follow!"

They had only gone a short distance when Little Peachling heard a pheasant calling, "Ken! ken! ken! Where are you off to, Master Peachling?"

Just as before, Little Peachling told the pheasant, "I am off to the island of the Oni. I plan to find their treasure and carry it away."

"What is that which I see you carrying?" asked the pheasant.

"I am carrying the very best millet dumplings in all of Japan. My old parents made them for me specially for this trip," answered Little Peachling.

"Just as I thought!" said the pheasant. "If you give me one of them, I will go along with you."

Little Peachling took out one of his dumplings and gave it to the pheasant. The pheasant eagerly took it and said, "Lead, Little Peachling, and I will follow!"

A little while after this, they met a dog who cried, "Bow! wow! wow! Whither are you going, Master Peachling?"

Just as before, Little Peachling told the dog, "I am off to the island of the Oni. I plan to find their treasure and carry it away."

"What is that which I see you carrying?" asked the dog.

"I am carrying the very best millet dumplings in all of Japan. My old parents made them for me specially for this trip," answered Little Peachling.

"If you will give me one of those nice millet dumplings of yours, I will go along with you," said the dog.

"With all of my heart," said Little Peachling as he gave a dumpling to the dog.

The dog took it eagerly and said, "Lead, Little Peachling, and I will follow!"

So Little Peachling went on his way with the monkey, the pheasant, and the dog following after him.

When they got to the Oni's island, the pheasant flew over the castle gate and the monkey scampered over the castle wall. Little Peachling, leading the dog, forced the gate and got into the castle. They did battle with the Oni and put them to flight. They even took the Oni king as prisoner.

With that, all of the Oni did homage to Little Peachling and brought out the treasures they had hoarded. Among the treasures were caps and coats that made their wearers invisible and jewels that governed the ebb and flow of the tide. There also were coral, musk, emeralds, amber, and tortoiseshell besides gold and silver. All of these were laid before Little Peachling by the conquered Oni.

And so, in ancient days in a remote part of Japan, Little Peachling went home loaded with riches. He and his parents lived in peace and plenty for the rest of their lives.

The Pear Tree

(China)

IT WAS THE EIGHTH DAY OF THE TWELFTH MOON and the sun was shining brightly. A fruit peddler was pushing his wagon at the side of the road, which ran between two large towns. It was a very busy road with many people going and coming.

This peddler was stingy and greedy. He had tied an umbrella to the top of a pole so that it shaded his baskets of juicy brown pears. "This road is a good place to sell my pears. Because it is such a hot day, travelers will be thirsty. I am sure that I will sell every one of my luscious pears."

Just as on every busy road, the people using it were of all kinds. Some had money and some were poor. The one thing they had in common was their thirst, because it was such a hot day. Those who could spare the money bought pears and smacked their lips as they ate them. Those who could not spare the money could only look longingly at the baskets of fruit on the wagon in the shade of the umbrella.

In the middle of the afternoon, an old man who was dressed like a farmer came along. He had on a blue jacket and dusty, dirty blue pants. He looked as if he had just come from working in his fields. He carried a hoe over his shoulder and looked quite tired. It looked as though he had let the rains wash his face and the winds comb his hair for him.

If you really looked closely and examined this old man, though, there was something strange about him. His eyes were sparkling and his face looked different from those of the other farmers. The stingy fruit peddler ignored the old man because he thought that the old man was shabby and too poor to buy any pears.

The old man came up to the wagon of the pear seller and said, "Oh honorable fruit peddler, I am thirsty. Even though I do not have any money to buy your pears, I feel certain that you are a man of kindness and will spare a pear for a man of such great age as mine."

The unfriendly fruit peddler cried, "Leave me, you worthless beggar. I sell my pears, I do not give them away. If I gave them away to every useless person who stopped by my wagon I would have nothing to sell. Go away!"

The old farmer looked steadily at the peddler. "I am old. My mouth waters for a pear. I do not expect to have you give me a fine pear, just one of the poorest, smallest ones from your baskets. If you do so, I will bring blessings upon you."

"I told you once to go away. Go away! I do not need your blessings, you old goat. I should beat you for bothering me!" shouted the fruit peddler. In fact, the peddler became so loud and threatening a crowd gathered around his wagon.

Bystanders called out, "For shame. This farmer is old and weary. He is thirsty and poor. Give him a pear. One small pear won't be missed by you. You could make the old man's life a bit more pleasant with only one pear!" Everyone in the crowd murmured agreement.

"Well, that is easy for you to say," cried the angry peddler. "You are very generous with my property. If you care so much for this old man, why don't you buy a pear for him with your own money?"

The same bystander who had spoken first laid down a few coins and selected a big pear from the fruit peddler's basket. "Here, old man. Take this pear and enjoy!"

The old man took it with a bow and thanked the man very politely. The old man looked so different, the people lingered while he ate the pear down to the core. It was as if the people wanted to see what would happen next. And they did. The old man picked out all of the seeds and turned them over and over in the palm of his hand. After examining the seeds, he selected one and threw the others away.

"I will now show you something that you have perhaps never seen before and which may amuse you. You have been so kind to me, honorable gentlemen," the old man said to the crowd.

He took up his hoe and dug a hole in the ground. In this hole he placed the seed that he had so carefully chosen. He scattered the loose earth over it and pressed it down with his foot. "The next thing I need is a pot of hot water," he said. "Does anyone know where I might get such a thing?"

The crowd standing around him was quite curious by this time. One young man who was fond of a good joke lived close by. He ran and brought a kettle from his own kitchen.

The old farmer carefully sprinkled the earth with the hot water. In less time than it takes to tell about it, a tiny green shoot appeared in the earth where the seed had been planted. A few moments more and it was a pear tree almost a foot high. As the crowd, which was not quiet, stood by, it grew and it grew until it was as tall as a good sturdy pear tree. Before their very eyes, the people saw buds appear. The tree burst into fragrant bloom. The blossoms fell off and the fruit formed as they watched. The little pears swelled and swelled. They grew brown and soft and ripe.

While all of this was happening, the crowd had grown until it blocked the road. More and more people appeared as the news of this strange happening spread throughout the neighborhood.

The old farmer looked up at the tree and then at some young fellows in the crowd. "You young lads need to climb up the tree. Pick the ripe fruit and hand it down to us thirsty ones."

The young men did as he said and in no time they had stripped the branches. Everyone in the crowd was enjoying the taste of the juicy pears. Even the stingy peddler! He had joined the crowd and left his wagon to watch what happened and eat fruit from the amazing pear tree.

After everyone had eaten, the old farmer raised his hoe and with two or three blows he cut down the pear tree. It fell to the ground as the crowd watched. Its leaves seemed to shrivel and its branches grow smaller. At last the only part left was the slender tree trunk.

The old farmer picked this slender trunk up and used it as a staff. He leaned upon it and went on his way with a low bow to the crowd. The crowd was silent with wonder. It had all happened so quickly that they could scarcely believe that it had happened at all. The proof of it all was that each of them still held the cores of the pears they had eaten in their hands.

"My pears! My pears!" came the screams from the stingy fruit peddler. "They have all disappeared. All my money has been spent for those pears and now they are gone! It was that wretched farmer. He must have been a fairy. Ai, ai, it must have been my pears he used to appear in his wonderful tree."

One of the bystanders said, “If that is true, the old man rewarded you well. You treated him so poorly.” But the peddler never heard what was said because he was running along the road as hard as he could in search of the old farmer. The only thing that the peddler found was the old farmer’s staff, the trunk of the pear tree. It was then that the peddler saw that the staff was really the pole that he had tied his umbrella to for shade.

Surely the old man was a fairy who had taken the form of a farmer. Perhaps he had been sent just to give the stingy peddler a lesson in good behavior.

The Hungry Wolf
(Estonia)

IN THE OLD, OLD DAYS the wolf was by no means the wicked, wild beast he is now. He was as tame as our dogs are.

Once, however, a farmer's wife threw to a wolf, instead of his usual food, a red-hot stone. The wolf ran away from men and from this day on became the malicious beast he is.

The hot stone burned the wolf's jaws. For some time he and all his comrades received their food from heaven. But it came to pass that one day at mealtime, one wolf was overlooked and left without food. He complained bitterly of this injustice.

"Eat him whom you meet first!" was the response to the wolf's complaint.

The hungry wolf tripped away in search of his food. Soon he met a ragged, skinny beggar. "I received orders from heaven to eat you!" barked the wolf.

"Dear wolf," prayed the beggar, "a poor morsel I would make for you. Just a heap of worthless old bones. Better wait for a younger and tastier mouthful!"

"Quite right!" thought the wolf to himself. "An old creature like this is worth nothing. I shall rather look for a real tidbit."

So graciously he said to the beggar, "I grant your wish. Go!"

On and on ran the wolf. This time he met a woman. "I shall devour you!" barked the wolf.

The woman shrieked and wailed, "Oh, good dear wolf, spare my life! I have little children at home. Who is to care for them if you kill me?"

"Now what am I to do?" thought the wolf. His stomach was more than empty and noisily demanded food. But he was moved to the depths of his heart by the pleas of the woman.

"Go back and live in peace with your children!" he said at last.

Onward and onward trotted the hungry wolf in his search. Soon he encountered a sturdy young man. The wolf halted before the young man and said, "I have orders from heaven to devour you. Be prepared! I shall begin at once."

"If it is so ordered from heaven, I must obey. Eat me if you must! But before you start, let me measure if there is enough room for me in your stomach."

"But how will you do the measuring?"

"With the measuring stick, of course!"

The young man went and cut a good-sized cudgel from a bush by the roadside. After this he took off his belt.

"What are you going to do with this?" questioned the puzzled wolf.

"I am taking it off because it might prevent me from lying comfortably in your stomach. Here, take it! I present it to you!"

Here the young man tied one end of his belt to the wolf's leg, the other end to the trunk of a big tree. "Now the measuring begins," he exclaimed. Immediately heavy blows began to fall, as fast as hail, upon the wolf's back.

The poor beast tried to free himself and flee, but could not. "Dear friend, do not beat me any longer! I shall never eat you! I never for an instant meant it in earnest!" begged the wolf.

"Whether you eat me or not, a good tanning you must get just the same!" And the young man measured and measured the wolf's sides until all the fur came off. The wolf jerked and jumped about, howling with rage and pain. At last the belt broke and the wolf was lucky enough to escape.

When he returned to the woods he complained of his ill luck to his comrades and a whole pack of wolves decided to go to punish the insolent young man. And they went.

When the young man noticed the approach of the wolves he knew he was in great danger. Quick as a flash he rushed up a big tree.

The angry wolves gathered under the tree and snarled at the young man fiercely. But they were unable to reach him. Then they held a council of war.

The wolf who had been beaten proposed, "Let us all lie down, one upon the other, so that the pile made by our bodies would be high enough for our topmost brother to reach the offender." The whole pack was pleased with this plan.

The beaten wolf laid himself down first. The rest climbed one upon another's back and the heap grew higher and higher until it was high enough to reach their victim.

Suddenly the young man shouted in defiance, "Just you wait, Beaten Sides! I tanned your hide once but you will get some more tanning now!"

At these words the beaten wolf sprang up in terror and fled. The whole pile of wolves tumbled down, some breaking their necks, others their legs or ribs. They all ran for their lives and vanished into the woods, following the example set by Beaten Sides.

The young man came down the tree and continued peacefully on his way. And the wolves abandoned forever thoughts of vengeance against him.

Ever since that day, the wolf runs away when he meets a man, but the sight of sheep still makes him furious, because the belt with which Beaten Sides was fastened to the tree trunk was woven of sheep's wool.

The Wonderful Pig
(Hungary)

IN A FARAWAY LAND, where the goose thrashes the corn with its wings and the goat grinds the flour with its chin, there was a princess who was very beautiful but very eccentric. She announced publicly that she would only marry the man who could tell her father, the king, a story that he could not believe.

Now in a village there dwelt a poor young peasant who, hearing of this proclamation, went up to the king's palace and loudly knocked at the gates, demanding an audience with his majesty.

The king knew very well what the young fellow wanted, as by that time many princes and knights had come on the same errand, in the hope of winning the beautiful princess, but they all had failed.

So John, the young peasant, was admitted to the royal presence. "Good morning, your majesty," he said.

"Good morning, my lad. Well, what do you want?" asked the king kindly.

"So please your majesty, I want a wife."

"Very good, lad. What would you keep her on?"

"Oh! I dare say I could manage to keep her pretty comfortably. My father has a pig."

"Indeed!" said the king.

"A wonderful pig, your majesty. He has kept my father, my mother, seven sisters, and myself for the last twenty years."

"Indeed!" said the king.

"He gives us as good a quart of milk every morning as any cow."

"Indeed!" said the king.

"Yes, your majesty, and lays most delicious eggs for our breakfast."

"Indeed!" said the king.

"And every day my mother cuts a nice bit of bacon out of his side, and every night it grows together again."

"Indeed!" said the king.

"The other day this pig disappeared, and my mother looked for him high and low. He was nowhere to be seen."

"That was very sad," said the king.

"Finally she found him in the larder, catching mice."

"A very useful pig!" said the king.

"My father sent him into town every day to do errands for him."

"Very wise of your father," said the king.

"He ordered all my father's clothes, aye, and mine too, of your majesty's own tailor."

"They do appear very well made!" said the king.

"Yes, your majesty. The pig also pays all the bills out of the gold he picks up on the road."

"A very precious pig," said the king.

"Lately he has seemed unruly and rather out of sorts."

"That's very sad!" said the king.

"He has refused to go where he is told and won't allow my mother to have any more bacon from his side."

"He should be chastised!" said the king.

"Besides which, your majesty, he is growing rather blind and can't see where he is going."

"He should be led," said the king.

"Yes, your majesty, that is why my father has just engaged your father to look after him."

"That's not true," yelled the king ... then suddenly he remembered his daughter's promise. So he was obliged to allow the princess to marry the peasant's son, but this he never regretted, for the peasant's son became a most clever and amiable young prince. He lived happily with his bride and his father-in-law for many, many years. Years after, when John became the king, all his people declared that they had never had so wise a ruler. Then it was that he imagined no longer but was always believed and respected.

Jack and the Beanstalk
(England)

ONCE UPON A TIME, there was a poor widow who had an only son named Jack, and a cow named Milky-white. All they had to live on was the milk the cow gave every morning, which they carried to the market and sold. But one morning Milky-white gave no milk and they didn't know what to do.

"What shall we do, what shall we do?" said the widow, wringing her hands.

"Cheer up, Mother, I'll go and get work somewhere," said Jack.

"We've tried that before, and nobody would take you," said his mother. "We must sell Milky-white and with the money start a shop or something."

"All right, Mother," said Jack. "It is market day today and I'll soon sell Milky-white and then we'll see what we can do."

So he took the cow's halter in his hand, and off he started. He hadn't gone far when he met a funny-looking old man who said to him, "Good morning, Jack."

"Good morning to you," said Jack and wondered how this old fellow knew his name.

"Well, Jack, and where are you off to?" said the man.

"I'm going to market to sell our cow here."

"Oh, you look the proper sort of chap to sell cows," said the man. "I wonder if you know how many beans make five."

"Two in each hand and one in your mouth," said Jack, as sharp as a needle.

"Right you are," said the man. "Here they are, the very beans themselves," he went on, pulling out of his pocket a number of strange-looking beans. "As you are so sharp," says he, "I don't mind doing a swap with you—your cow for these beans."

"Go along," says Jack. "Wouldn't you like it!"

"Ah, you don't know what these beans are," said the man. "If you plant them overnight, by morning, they grow right up to the sky."

"Really?" says Jack. "You don't say so!"

"Yes, that is so, and if it doesn't turn out to be true you can have your cow back."

"Right," says Jack, hands him over Milky-white's halter, and pockets the beans.

Back goes Jack home, and as he hadn't gone very far it wasn't dusk by the time he got to his door.

"Back already, Jack?" said his mother. "I see you haven't got Milky-white, so you've sold her. How much did you get for her?"

"You'll never guess, Mother," says Jack.

"No, you don't say so. Good boy! Five pounds, ten, fifteen, no, it can't be twenty."

"I told you that you couldn't guess. What do you say to these beans! They are magical. Plant them and overnight—"

"What?" says Jack's mother. "Have you been such a fool, such a dolt, such an idiot, as to give away my Milky-white, the best milker in the parish, and prime beef to boot, for a set of paltry beans. Take that! Take that! Take that! For your precious beans here they go out of the window! Now, off with you to bed. Not a sup shall you drink and not a bit shall you swallow this very night."

So Jack went upstairs to his little room in the attic, and sad and sorry he was, to be sure, as much for his mother's sake as for the loss of his supper.

At last he dropped off to sleep.

When he woke up, the room looked so funny. The sun was shining into part of it, and yet all the rest was quite dark and shady. So Jack jumped up and dressed himself and went to the window. What do you think he saw? Why, the beans his mother had thrown out of the window into the garden had sprung up into a big beanstalk that went up and up and up till it reached the sky. So the man spoke the truth after all.

The beanstalk grew up quite close past Jack's window, so all he had to do was to open it and give a jump onto the beanstalk, which ran up just like a big ladder. Jack climbed, and he climbed, and he climbed till at last he reached the sky. When he got there he found a long, broad road going as straight as a dart. He walked along and he walked along and he walked along till he came to a great big tall house, and on the doorstep there was a great big tall woman.

"Good morning, mum," says Jack, quite polite-like. "Could you be so kind as to give me some breakfast?" He hadn't had anything to eat the night before, you remember, and he was as hungry as a hunter.

"It's breakfast you want, is it?" says the great big tall woman. "It's breakfast you'll be if you don't move off from here. My man is an ogre and there's nothing he likes better than boys broiled on toast. You'd better be moving on or he'll soon be coming."

"Oh! Please, mum, do give me something to eat, mum. I've had nothing to eat since yesterday morning, really and truly, mum," says Jack. "I may as well be broiled as die of hunger."

Well, the ogre's wife was not half so bad after all. She took Jack into the kitchen and gave him a hunk of bread and cheese and a jug of milk. Jack hadn't half finished these when thump! thump! thump! the whole house began to tremble with the noise of someone coming.

"Goodness gracious me! It is my old man," said the ogre's wife. "What on earth shall I do? Come along quick and jump in here." She bundled Jack into the oven just as the ogre came in.

He was a big one, to be sure. At his belt he had three calves strung up by the heels, and he unhooked them and threw them down on the table and said, "Here, Wife, broil me a couple of these for breakfast. Ah! What's this I smell?

Fee-fi-fo-fum,
I smell the blood of an Englishman,
Be he alive or be he dead
I'll have his bones to grind my bread.

"Nonsense, dear," said his wife. "You are dreaming. Or perhaps you smell the scraps of that little boy you liked so much for yesterday's dinner. Here you go and have a wash and tidy up. By the time you come back your breakfast will be ready for you."

So off went the ogre, and Jack was just going to jump out of the oven and run away when the woman told him not to. "Wait till he's asleep," says she. "He always has a doze after breakfast."

Well, the ogre had his breakfast. After that he goes to a big chest and takes out of it a couple of bags of gold, and down he sits and counts till at last his head begins to nod. He began to snore till the whole house shook again.

Then Jack crept out on tiptoe from his oven and as he was passing the ogre he took one of the bags of gold under his arm. Off he peltered till he came to the beanstalk. He threw down the bag of gold, which of course fell into his mother's garden. Then he climbed down till at last he got home and told his mother and showed her the gold and said, "Well, Mother, wasn't I right about the beans? They are really magical, you see."

So they lived on the bag of gold for some time, but at last they came to the end of it. Jack made up his mind to try his luck once more up at the top of the beanstalk. One fine morning he rose up early and got onto the beanstalk, and he climbed and he climbed and he climbed and he climbed and he climbed and he climbed till at last he came out onto the road again and up to the great big tall house he had been to before. There, sure enough, was the great big tall woman a-standing on the doorstep.

"Good morning, mum," says Jack as bold as brass. "Could you be so good as to give me something to eat?"

"Go away, my boy," said the big tall woman, "or else my man will eat you up for breakfast. Aren't you the youngster who came here once before? Do you know, that very day, my man missed one of his bags of gold?"

"That's strange, mum," says Jack. "I dare say I could tell you something about that, but I'm so hungry I can't speak till I've had something to eat."

Well, the big tall woman was so curious that she took him in and gave him something to eat. He had scarcely begun munching it as slowly as he could when thump! thump! thump! they heard the giant's footstep. The wife hid Jack away in the oven again.

All happened as it did before. In came the ogre as he did before, said,

Fee-fi-fo-fum,
I smell the blood of an Englishman,
Be he alive, or be he dead
I'll have his bones to grind my bread.

The giant had his breakfast of three broiled oxen. Then he said to his wife, "Wife, bring me the hen that lays the golden eggs." So she brought it, and the ogre said, "Lay," and it laid an egg all of gold. Then the ogre began to nod his head and to snore till the house shook.

Then Jack crept out of the oven on tiptoe and caught hold of the golden hen and was off before you could say "Jack Robinson." But this time the hen gave a cackle that woke the ogre and just as Jack got out of the house he heard him calling, "Wife, Wife, what have you done with my golden hen?"

The wife said, "Why, my dear?"

But that was all Jack heard, for he rushed off to the beanstalk and climbed down like a house on fire. When he got home he showed his mother the wonderful hen and said, "Lay," to it. It laid a golden egg every time he said, "Lay."

Jack was not content, and it wasn't very long before he determined to have another try at his luck up there at the top of the beanstalk. One fine morning, he rose up early and got onto the beanstalk, and he climbed and he climbed and he climbed and he climbed till he got to the top. This time he knew better than to go straight to the ogre's house. When he got near it he waited behind a bush till he saw the ogre's wife come out with a pail to get some water. He crept into the house and got into the copper. He hadn't been there long when he heard thump! thump! thump! as before. In came the ogre and his Wife.

"Fee-fi-fo-fum, I smell the blood of an Englishman," cried out the ogre. "I smell him, Wife, I smell him."

"Do you, my dearie?" says the ogre's wife. "Then if it's that little rogue that stole your gold and the hen that laid the golden egg, he's sure to have got into the oven." They both rushed to the oven. But Jack wasn't there, luckily, and the ogre's wife said, "There you are again with your fee-fi-fo-fum. Why of course it's the boy you caught last night that I've just broiled for your breakfast. How forgetful I am. How careless you are not to know the difference between live and dead after all these years."

So the ogre sat down to the breakfast and ate it, but every now and then he would mutter, "Well, I could have sworn—" and he'd get up and search the larder and the cupboards and everything, only luckily he didn't think of the copper.

After breakfast was over, the ogre called out, "Wife, Wife, bring me my golden harp." She brought it and put it on the table before him. Then he said, "Sing!" and the golden harp sang most beautifully. And it went on singing till the ogre fell asleep, and commenced to snore like thunder.

Then Jack lifted up the copper-lid very quietly and got down like a mouse and crept on hands and knees till he came to the table, where up he crawled, caught hold of the golden harp, and dashed with it toward the door. But the harp called out quite loud, "Master! Master!" The ogre woke up just in time to see Jack running off with his harp.

Jack ran as fast as he could and the ogre came rushing after and would soon have caught him, only Jack had a start and dodged him a bit and knew where he was going. When he got to the beanstalk the ogre was not more than twenty yards away, when suddenly he saw Jack disappear, and when he came to the end of the road he saw Jack underneath climbing down for dear life. Well, the ogre didn't like trusting himself to such a ladder, and he stood and waited, so Jack got another start. But just then the harp cried out, "Master! Master!" and the ogre swung himself down onto the beanstalk, which shook with his weight. Down climbed Jack and after him climbed the ogre. By this time Jack had climbed down and climbed down and climbed down till he was very nearly home.

He called out, "Mother! Mother! Bring me an ax, bring me an ax!"

His mother came rushing out with the ax in her hand. When she came to the beanstalk she stood stock-still with fright, for there she saw the ogre with his legs just through the clouds.

Jack jumped down and got hold of the ax and gave a chop at the beanstalk that cut it almost in half. The ogre felt the beanstalk shake and quiver, so he stopped to see what was the matter. Then Jack gave another chop with the ax and the beanstalk was cut in two and began to topple over. The ogre fell down and broke his crown, and the beanstalk came toppling after.

Then Jack showed his mother his golden harp, and what with showing that and selling the golden eggs, Jack and his mother became very rich. He married a great princess and they lived happily ever after.

Scrapefoot
(England)

ONCE UPON A TIME, there were three Bears who lived in a castle in a great wood. One of them was a great big Bear, and one was a middling Bear, and one was a little Bear. In the same wood there was a fox who lived all alone, whose name was Scrapefoot. Scrapefoot was very much afraid of the Bears, but for all that he wanted very much to know all about them. And one day as he went through the wood he found himself near the Bears' Castle, and he wondered whether he could get into the castle. He looked all about him everywhere, and he could not see anyone. So he came up very quietly, till at last he came up to the door of the castle, and he tried whether he could open it. Yes! The door was not locked, and he opened it just a little way, and put his nose in and looked, and he could not see anyone. So then he opened it a little way farther, and put one paw in, and then another paw, and another and another, and then he was all in the Bears' Castle. He found he was in a great hall with three chairs in it—one big, one middling, and one little chair. He thought he would like to sit down and rest and look about him. He sat down on the big chair. But he found it so hard and uncomfortable that it made his bones ache, and he jumped down at once and got into the middling chair. He turned round and round in it, but he couldn't make himself comfortable. Then he went to the little chair and sat down in it, and it was so soft and warm and comfortable that Scrapefoot was quite happy. All at once it broke to pieces under him and he couldn't put it together again!

He got up and began to look about him again, and on one table he saw three saucers, of which one was very big, one middling, and one quite little. Scrapefoot was very thirsty, and he began to drink out of the big saucer, which was so sour and so nasty that he would not taste another drop of it. Then he tried the middling saucer and he drank a little of that. He tried two or three mouthfuls, but it was not nice. Then he left it and went to the little saucer, and the milk in the little saucer was so sweet and so nice that he went on drinking it till it was all gone.

Then Scrapefoot thought he would like to go upstairs. He listened and he could not hear anyone. So upstairs he went. He found a great room with three beds in it. One was a big bed and one was a middling bed, and one was a little white bed. He climbed up into the big bed, but it was so hard and lumpy and uncomfortable that he jumped down again at once and tried the middling bed. That was rather better, but he could not get comfortable in it, so after turning about a little while he got up and went to the little bed. That was so soft and so warm and so nice that he fell fast asleep at once.

After a time the Bears came home. When they got into the hall the big Bear went to his chair and said, "Who's been sitting in my chair?" The middling Bear said, "Who's been sitting in my chair?" The little Bear said, "Who's been sitting in my chair and has broken it all to pieces?" They went to have their milk and the big Bear said, "Who's been drinking my milk?" and the middling Bear said, "Who's been drinking my milk?" The little Bear said, "Who's been drinking my milk and has drunk it all up?" Then they went upstairs and into the bedroom and the big Bear said, "Who's been sleeping in my bed?" and the middling Bear said, "Who's been sleeping in my bed?" The little Bear said, "Who's been sleeping in my bed?—and here he is!"

The Bears wondered what they should do with the fox. The big Bear said, "Let's hang him!" The middling Bear said, "Let's drown him!" The little Bear said, "Let's throw him out of the window." Then the Bears took him to the window and the big Bear took two legs on one side and the middling Bear took two legs on the other side and they swung him backwards and forwards, backwards and forwards, and out of the window.

Poor Scrapefoot was very frightened and he thought every bone in his body must be broken. He got up and first shook one leg—no, that was not broken. Then another, and that was not broken. Another and another, and then he wagged his tail and found there were no bones broken. So then he galloped off home as fast as he could go, and never went near the Bears' Castle again.

The Story of the Three Bears
(England)

Once upon a time, there were Three Bears who lived together in a house of their own, in a wood. One of them was a Little, Small, Wee Bear. One was a Middle-sized Bear, and the other was a Great, Huge Bear. They had each a pot for their porridge, a little pot for the Little, Small, Wee Bear, a middle-sized pot for the Middle-sized Bear, and a great pot for the Great, Huge Bear. They each had a chair to sit in. A little chair for the Little, Small, Wee Bear, a middle-sized chair for the Middle-sized Bear, and a great chair for the Great, Huge Bear. They each had a bed to sleep in. A little bed for the Little, Small, Wee Bear, a middle-sized bed for the Middle-sized Bear, and a great bed for the Great, Huge Bear.

One day, after they had made the porridge for their breakfast and poured it into their porridge pots, they walked out into the wood while the porridge was cooling that they might not burn their mouths by beginning too soon to eat it.

While they were walking, a little old Woman came to the house. She could not have been a good, honest old Woman, for first she looked in at the window. Then she peeped in at the keyhole. Seeing nobody in the house, she lifted the latch. The door was not fastened because the Bears were good Bears who did nobody any harm and never suspected that anybody would harm them.

The little old Woman opened the door and went in. She was well pleased when she saw the porridge on the table. If she had been a good little old Woman, she would have waited till the Bears came home, and then perhaps they would have asked her to breakfast. They were good Bears, a little rough or so, as the manner of Bears is, but for all that, very good-natured and hospitable. But she was an impudent, bad old Woman and set about helping herself.

First she tasted the porridge of the Great, Huge Bear and that was too hot for her. She said a bad word about that! Then she tasted the porridge of the Middle-sized Bear and that was too cold for her. She said a bad word about that, too! She went to the porridge of the Little, Small, Wee Bear, and tasted that. That was neither too hot, nor too cold, but just right. She liked it so well that she ate it all up. The naughty old Woman said a bad word about the little porridge pot because it did not hold enough for her.

Then the little old Woman sat down in the chair of the Great, Huge Bear and that was too hard for her. Then she sat down in the chair of the Middle-sized Bear and that was too soft for her. She sat down in the chair of the Little, Small, Wee Bear and that was neither too hard nor too soft but just right. So she seated herself in it and there she sat till the bottom of the chair came out and down she came, plump upon the ground. The naughty Woman said a wicked word about that too.

Then the little old Woman went upstairs into the bed chamber in which the Three Bears slept. First she lay down upon the bed of the Great, Huge Bear, but that was too high at the head for her. Next, she lay down upon the bed of the Middle-sized Bear. That was too high at the foot for her. She lay down upon the bed of the Little, Small, Wee Bear, and that was neither too high at the head nor at the foot but just right. She covered herself up comfortably and lay there till she fell fast asleep.

By this time the Three Bears thought their porridge would be cool enough, so they came home to breakfast. The little old Woman had left the spoon of the Great, Huge Bear standing in his porridge.

"Somebody has been at my porridge!"said the Great, Huge Bear, in his great, rough, gruff voice. When the Middle-sized Bear looked at its bowl, it saw that the spoon was standing in it too. They were wooden spoons. If they had been silver ones, the naughty old Woman would have put them in her pocket.

"Somebody has been at my porridge!" said the Middle-sized Bear in a middle-sized voice.

Then the Little, Small, Wee Bear looked at his and there was the spoon in the porridge pot, but the porridge was all gone. "Somebody has been at my porridge and has eaten it all up!" said the Little, Small, Wee Bear, in his little, small, wee voice.

Upon this the Three Bears, seeing that someone had entered their house and eaten up the Little, Small, Wee Bear's breakfast, began to look about them. The little old Woman had not put the hard cushion straight when she rose from the chair of the Great, Huge Bear.

"Somebody has been sitting in my chair!" said the Great, Huge Bear in his great, rough, gruff voice.

And the little old Woman had squatted down the soft cushion of the Middle-sized Bear.

"Somebody has been sitting in my chair!" said the Middle-sized Bear in a middle-sized voice.

You know what the little old Woman had done to the third chair.

"Somebody has been sitting in my chair and has sat the bottom out of it!" said the Little, Small, Wee Bear in his little, small, wee voice.

Then the Three Bears went upstairs into their bed chamber. The little old Woman had pulled the pillow of the Great, Huge Bear out of its place.

"Somebody has been lying in my bed!" said the Great, Huge Bear, in his great, rough, gruff voice.

The little old Woman had pulled the bolster of the Middle-sized Bear out of its place.

"Somebody has been lying in my bed!" said the Middle-sized Bear in a middle-sized voice.

When the Little, Small, Wee Bear came to look at his bed, there was the bolster in its place. The pillow was in its place upon the bolster. Upon the pillow was the little old Woman's ugly, dirty head, which was not in its place, for she had no business there.

"Somebody has been lying in my bed—and here she is!" said the Little, Small, Wee Bear, in his little, small, wee voice.

The little old Woman had heard in her sleep the great, rough, gruff voice of the Great, Huge Bear, but she was so fast asleep that it was no more to her than the roaring of wind or the rumbling of thunder. She had heard the middle-sized voice of the Middle-sized Bear but it was only as if she had heard someone speaking in a dream. When she heard the little, small, wee voice of the Little, Small, Wee Bear, it was so sharp and so shrill that it awakened her at once. Up she started and when she saw the Three Bears on one side of the bed, she tumbled herself out the other and ran to the window. Now the window was open because the Bears, like good, tidy Bears, as they were, always opened their bed chamber window when they got up in the morning.

Out the little old Woman jumped. Whether she broke her neck in the fall or ran into the wood and was lost there or found her way out of the wood and was taken up by the constable and sent to the House of Correction for a vagrant as she was, I cannot tell. But the Three Bears never saw anything more of her.

Food for Thought

- ▲ Create and tell a story about a meal you would like to be invited to as a guest. What foods would be served? Who would be sharing this meal with you? Where would it take place?
- ▲ Find a copy of *Carrot Seed* by Ruth Krauss (New York: Harper Collins Childrens Books, 1973). Rewrite this story into reader's theater format. Have a group of friends share it with the class.
- ▲ There are variants of "The North Wind" among the Irish and English and in the Bahamas and in Richard Chase's *Jack Tales* (New York: Houghton Mifflin Co., 1943). Locate some of these other versions in the library. The magical objects and animals vary considerably in these tales. Make a chart showing how the different tales are similar to and different from "The North Wind."
- ▲ Invent a new, unique food. Write or tell a story in which this food plays an important part. Create your own recipe for this new food. Make the recipe and try it out on friends and family. Be sure to tell them the story behind it.
- ▲ The author Robert Southey based his story "The Three Bears" on a story that existed in all countries of Europe, a series of beast tales relating to the feud between the Fox and the Bear. "Scrapefoot" is an example of one of the beast tales. Find a version of "Goldilocks" and compare these three stories. How are they alike and different? Which story is most appealing? Why?

- Refer to "Goldilocks and the Three Bears" and "Jack and the Beanstalk" in *Storybook Stew* by Suzanne I. Barchers and Peter J. Rauen (Golden, Colo.: Fulcrum, 1996) for more ideas.
- Tell or read one of the stories in this section to a group of younger students. Watch to see how they react to the story. Lead a discussion with them on the part food plays in the story.
- Ask an older family member to tell you about a time when you were convinced that something that had happened was magic. Share what you discover with others. Using the information, create a story using the story that your elder told you. You should add elements from your own imagination to enhance the story.
- Ask an older family member to tell you a story about something that happened to you as a youngster that involved food. Was this a funny, exciting, or frightening incident? Can you develop this into a personal story to share with others?
- Collect comic strips you find that are related to eating and food. Develop categories for these strips and share them with others. Or you can create your own comic strip that focuses on food. You may borrow ideas from the stories that you have just read. Think about what superpowers the hero and the villain of the cartoon should have that would relate to an aspect of food (e.g., Spaghetti Man shoots meatballs at villains to knock them down and uses extra-strong vermicelli as a lasso).

Bibliography

Aliki. *A Medieval Feast*. New York: Harper & Row, 1983.
Depicts all the preparation and entertainment for a feast fit for medieval royalty.

Barchers, Suzanne I. *Wise Women*. Englewood, Colo.: Libraries Unlimited, 1990.
Folk and fairy tales from around the world devoted to heroines with spunk.

Barchers, Suzanne I., and Peter J. Rauen. *Storybook Stew*. Golden, Colo.: Fulcrum Publishing, 1996.
Fifty recipes for different meals, each recipe accompanied by a summary of a featured book and a suggested activity.

Barton, Byron. *The Three Bears*. New York: HarperCollins, 1991.
Another version of this classic story.

Brett, Jan. *Goldilocks and the Three Bears*. New York: G.P. Putnam's Sons, 1987.
A well-illustrated version of *Goldilocks*.

Brown, Marcia. *Stone Soup*. New York: Scribner's, 1975.
Illustrated by an award-winning artist.

Bruchac, Joseph. *Tell Me a Tale*. San Diego: Harcourt, Brace, 1997.
Storyteller Joseph Bruchac incorporates many of his favorite tales in this discussion of the four basic components of storytelling: listening, observing, remembering, and sharing.

Caulley, Lorinda Bryan. *The Pancake Boy*. New York: G.P. Putnam's Sons, 1988.
Another example of the classic pancake boy story.

Chase, Richard. *Jack Tales*. Boston: Houghton Mifflin, 1943.
Folktales from the Southern Appalachians are collected and retold by Chase. The book includes several variations on the theme seen in English stories.

Cook, Scott. *The Gingerbread Boy*. New York: Knopf, 1987.
Another escape attempt by the gingerbread boy.

dePaola, Tomie. *Strega Nona*. New York: Scholastic, 1975.
Strega Nona has a magic pasta pot, but Big Anthony starts the pot cooking with disastrous results.

De Regniers, Beatrice Schenk. *Jack and the Beanstalk*. New York: Aladdin Books, 1985.
A traditional variation of the story.

DeRegniers, Beatrice. *Jack the Giant-Killer*. New York: Atheneum, 1987.
Retells Jack's encounter with a giant, including such lore as the right way to shake hands with a giant.

Ehlert, Lois. *Growing Vegetable Soup*. San Diego: Harcourt & Brace, 1987.
Just how does one go about growing vegetable soup?

Faulkner, Matt. *Jack and the Beanstalk*. New York: Scholastic, 1986.
The classic tale of clever Jack, who climbs a beanstalk and outwits a hungry giant.

Galdone, Paul. *The Gingerbread Boy.* New York: Clarion, 1975.
The classic story of a little old woman and a little old man and their gingerbread boy.

———. *Jack and the Beanstalk*. New York: Clarion, 1974.
A fanciful version of the story set in rhyme, with a different twist.

———. *The Magic Porridge Pot*. Boston: Houghton Mifflin, 1976.
Another version of the classic story.

Garner, Alan. *Jack and the Beanstalk*. New York: Doubleday, 1992.
A boy climbs to the top of a giant beanstalk, where he uses his quick wits to outsmart a boy-eating ogre.

Haley, Gail E. *Jack and the Beantree*. New York: Crown, 1986.
Another version of Jack and the giant.

Haviland, Virginia. *The Talking Pot*. Boston: Little, Brown, 1971.
Clever telling of the classic pot story.

Kellogg, Steven. *Jack and the Beanstalk*. New York: Morrow, 1991.
The classic story of Jack, the beanstalk, and the giant.

Krauss, Ruth. *Carrot Seed*. New York: Harper & Row, 1945.
The wonderful story of a little boy and his success when he believes in the power of a single seed.

Livo, Norma J. *Who's Afraid ... ? Facing Children's Fears with Folktales*. Englewood, Colo.: Libraries Unlimited, 1994.
Many of the folktales included in this anthology involve food.

Livo, Norma J., and Dia Cha. *Folk Stories of the Hmong*. Englewood, Colo.: Libraries Unlimited, 1991.
This collection of stories of the Hmong from Southeast Asia contains stories of beliefs and traditions involving food.

Livo, Norma J., and Sandra A. Rietz. *Storytelling Activities*. Englewood, Colo.: Libraries Unlimited, 1987.

Many of the activities included can be adapted to enrich the stories related to food in *Moon Cakes to Maize.*

Marshall, James. *Goldilocks and the Three Bears.* New York: Dial Press, 1988.
Includes humorous illustrations of the classic story.

McGovern, Ann. *Stone Soup.* New York: Scholastic, 1968.
This is the basic telling of *Stone Soup.*

Mollel, Tololwa M. *Ananse's Feast.* New York: Clarion, 1997.
Ananse the spider is unwilling to share his feast. He tricks Akye the turtle so that he can eat all the food himself, but Akye finds a way to get even. This African story is full of humor.

Sawyer, Ruth. *Journey Cake, Ho!* New York: Viking, 1953.
Johnny leaves home to set out on his own with a journey cake that gets out of his pack and is chased by an assortment of animals.

Stevens, Janet. *Goldilocks and the Three Bears.* New York: Dial Press, 1988.
Stevens illustrates *Goldilocks* with her unique, humorous twist.

Temple, Frances. *Tiger Soup: An Anansi Story from Jamaica.* New York: Orchard, 1994.
Another Anansi story with Jamaican flavor.

Turkle, Brinton. *Deep in the Forest.* New York: Dutton, 1976.
A wordless picture book with outstanding illustrations of the Three Bears and the intruder.

Van Rynback, Iris. *The Soup Stone.* New York: Greenwillow, 1993.
Another version of *Stone Soup.*

Vigil, Angel. *The Corn Woman: Stories and Legends of the Hispanic Southwest.* Englewood, Colo.: Libraries Unlimited, 1994.
The title story is about a legend related to food.

Wolkstein, Diane. *The Magic Orange Tree and Other Haitian Folktales.* New York: Knopf, 1978.
A classic collection of stories with African roots from Haiti that include food.